With the whole outfit put together—the classic jewelry around her neck, the perilously high shoes adding a further four inches to her frame, the dress that clung in all the right places—she felt like a million dollars. And she felt even better when she saw the expression in his eyes as he stood watching her descend the staircase.

"Stop that," he said unsteadily, and Megan gathered herself sufficiently to answer.

"Stop what?"

"Looking so damned sexy. An outing to the theater doesn't stand a chance when your mouth is begging to be kissed...along with every other part of your body. Maybe," he growled, taking her into his arms, "we should just keep the taxi waiting a few minutes."

Megan laughed and touched the extravagant string of diamonds at her neck. "I'm not missing a minute of this play, Alessandro Caretti!"

"Are you telling me that I take second place in your life to a bunch of actors on a stage?"

She sighed. "I'm not your pro~~~~~~ Alessandr~~~

"When it c~~~~ sharing."

CATHY WILLIAMS was born in the West Indies and has been writing Harlequin romances for more than fifteen years. She is a great believer in the power of perseverance, as she had never written anything before (apart from school essays a lifetime ago!), and from the starting point of zero has now fulfilled her ambition to pursue this most enjoyable of careers. She would encourage any would-be writer to have faith and go for it!

She lives in the beautiful Warwickshire countryside with her husband and three children, Charlotte, Olivia and Emma. When not writing she is hard-pressed to find a moment's free time between the millions of household chores, not to mention being a one-woman taxi service for her daughters' never-ending social lives.

She derives inspiration from the hot, lazy, tropical island of Trinidad (where she was born), from the peaceful countryside of middle England and, of course, from her many friends, who are a rich source of plots and are particularly garrulous when it comes to describing Harlequin Presents® heroes. It would seem from their complaints that tall, dark and charismatic men are way too few and far between! Her hope is to continue writing romance fiction and providing those eternal tales of love for which, she feels, we all strive.

THE MULTI-MILLIONAIRE'S VIRGIN MISTRESS

CATHY WILLIAMS

~ LATIN LOVERS ~

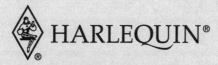

HARLEQUIN®

TORONTO • NEW YORK • LONDON
AMSTERDAM • PARIS • SYDNEY • HAMBURG
STOCKHOLM • ATHENS • TOKYO • MILAN • MADRID
PRAGUE • WARSAW • BUDAPEST • AUCKLAND

Recycling programs
for this product may
not exist in your area.

ISBN-13: 978-0-373-52754-0

THE MULTI-MILLIONAIRE'S VIRGIN MISTRESS

First North American Publication 2010.

Copyright © 2009 by Cathy Williams.

This edition published by arrangement with Harlequin Books S.A.

For questions and comments about the quality of this book please contact us at *Customer_eCare@Harlequin.ca*.

www.eHarlequin.com

Printed in U.S.A.

THE MULTI-MILLIONAIRE'S
VIRGIN MISTRESS

PROLOGUE

'WHAT the hell did you think you were playing at?'

Alessandro had stormed into the bedroom. There was no other way to put it. He had stormed into the bedroom. The beautiful, angular lines of his face were tight with anger and Megan didn't know why. Well, she sort of knew why. She just couldn't quite understand the depth of his fury.

'Playing at?' she asked weakly, hands clasped behind her back as she leant against the wall.

Having been practically shoved into the bedroom an hour before, like a stray bug that had inadvertently wandered into his bedsit, necessitating immediate quarantine, she had been on the verge of dozing off when the sound of his footsteps heading towards the room had seen her springing off the bed and virtually standing to attention by the window. Of course she had known that he wouldn't be sunshine and light, not after his reaction to her perfectly innocent and well-intentioned birthday surprise. She just hadn't reckoned on this backlash of anger.

'You heard me! That ridiculous stunt of yours!'

The voice that could make her weak with love and longing, that could drive her mad with desire, was cold and cutting.

'It wasn't a ridiculous stunt. It was a birthday surprise. I thought you'd *like* it.'

'*Like* you barging in unannounced and bursting out of a *birthday cake*? When I'm in the process of having a meeting with people who could change the direction of my life?'

Megan chewed her lip and stared at him. God, he was so beautiful. Even now, when he looked as though he would happily throttle her given half a chance, he was still sinfully sexy. Six foot two inches of gorgeous, head-turning masculinity, and all she wanted to do was coax him out of this black humour—because it *was* his birthday, after all, even if he had no desire to celebrate it.

She risked a little smile. 'You have no idea how strenuous it is being a birthday cake! I have the scars to prove it!' No exaggeration there, she thought. Her amazing plan had involved her friend Charlotte rigging up two boxes into something that resembled a cake—a piece of engineering which, Megan had been assured, would work like clockwork. One spring, and *bingo*! She would be revealed in all her glory! Her blonde curls had been tamed into a Marilyn Monroe format of soft waves, a mole had been perfectly positioned on one cheekbone, her full lips had been primed to scarlet, pouting perfection.

Needless to say they had not bargained on the full hour it had taken to be delivered in rush-hour traffic. Nor had they foreseen the possibility that the cunning contraption might prove to have a mind of its own, refusing to oblige a swift and easy exit, so that once in Alessandro's poky front room she had found herself having to do battle with masking tape when her legs were numb and her blood circulation virtually non-existent.

It had all added up to an inglorious, fairly shambolic situation, which had seen her crawling out of the box amidst a mass of screwed-up tape and crunched-up pink tissue paper—at which point she had been confronted by the embarrassing sight of three men in pinstriped suits and one very, very angry boyfriend.

'I was supposed to be Marilyn Monroe,' she expanded, when her smile failed to make headway.

She gestured to her outfit, which had started off in much better condition. Three hours before it had been a glamorous black swimsuit, revealing a tantalising amount of cleavage. She also wore high, black shoes, long black gloves and fishnet stockings. The swimsuit was still intact, but one glove was currently residing somewhere in said birthday cake, the shoes had been kicked off, and the fishnet tights now sported a long, unattractive rip down one leg. Not so much Marilyn-of-the-Happy-Birthday-Song as Marilyn-on-Tour-of-War-duty.

'I thought you'd be pleased.' Her voice was growing less confident by the second. 'Or at least find it funny.'

'Megan...' Alessandro sighed. 'We need to...to talk...'

She relaxed a little. Yes, she could do talking. He was the most fascinating man she had ever met, and she could talk to him until the cows came home—especially now, when he was no longer glaring at her with eyes that were like chips of dark, glacial ice.

'I guess we could...' she said, taking a couple steps towards him. 'Talk. Although...' a few more steps and she was standing directly in front of him, looking up at him '...I can think of more interesting things to do...' She splayed her hand across his chest, loving the feel of its rippling hardness. 'I prefer it when you wear shirts, Alessandro. I like unbuttoning them. Have I ever told you that? Tee shirts just aren't the same. Not that this black tee shirt doesn't look very nice on you.' It did. It wasn't baggy and shapeless, but clung in a very masculine way.

Alessandro reached out and caught her wandering hand in his. 'I said talk, Megan. And we can't *talk* in here.'

'Have your friends gone?'

'They weren't my *friends*.'

He dropped her hand and turned away, walking out of the bedroom so that she was obliged to follow him. He couldn't think straight when Megan was anywhere near the vicinity of a bed—especially when she was wearing an outfit that revealed every single curve of her fabulous, sexy little body.

'And put something on,' he commanded, without looking round.

'Oh, right. They're the people who are going to change the direction of your life.'

En route, she grabbed one of his shirts. He only wore white shirts, which she had told him was a very boring trait indeed. She had tried to even the balance by buying him a garishly coloured Hawaiian shirt, with a pattern of lurid coconut trees against a brilliant blue background, but he had yet to wear it. She suspected that it had been shoved at the bottom of his wardrobe somewhere.

She sensed him stiffen at her throwaway remark, but he didn't say anything. Just flung himself on the sofa that occupied one side of the space in his modest student accommodation, which only someone massively optimistic could call a *sitting room*.

It was literally a poky box, as he had told her on more than one occasion. But he had worked like a slave, he said, to put himself through university, and his destiny was to become master. Master of all he surveyed. Once he left, he would never look back

Megan didn't like to think too hard about where all of this mastery and conquering of the universe stuff was going to take him. Out of her life, she guessed. But who knew? Eternally optimistic, and madly in love for the very first time in her life, she was happy to put any thoughts about an uncertain future on hold. She was nineteen. She had her own college life to think about. She didn't want to foresee a day when her life wasn't going to be joined up with his.

'So who were they, anyway?' she asked now, settling on the sofa next to him and tucking her legs underneath her. She had to stop herself from reaching out and touching his face.

It still surprised and delighted her that she had been lucky enough to fall in love for the very first time with a man so absolutely perfect in every way. Her friends all led chaotic love-lives, constantly euphoric or depressed, or else hanging on the end of the line waiting for some guy to call. Alessandro had never done that. He had taken her virginity and cherished the gift she had given him, never taking her for granted or making promises he had no intention of fulfilling.

'They were…some fairly important people, Megan.'

He turned to look at her. Her hair was all over the place—soft, blonde hair, the colour of vanilla. Her cheeks were flushed, because he had obviously surprised her dozing. Only Megan could fall asleep in the space of seconds. Whilst wearing a ridiculous outfit. And after having made a complete fool of herself.

'Sorry,' she said in a contrite voice. Then, because she just couldn't help herself, she leaned towards him and stroked the side of his face with the back of his hand. 'I can understand why you were a bit put out when I appeared unannounced. Or should I say when I was brought in? Would have given anyone a shock. Especially an old man like you, Alessandro. Twenty-five years old! Practically over the hill! Do you realise it's just a matter of time before you're collecting your pension?'

She laughed, a rich, warm laugh which he had found infectious from the very first minute he had heard it across a crowded room, in a club to which he had been dragged by one of his colleagues at university who'd seemed to think he needed a break from his books. Every time he heard that laugh, which was often, he wanted to smile. Not, however, now.

'Here's how it was supposed to go. In an ideal world I would have made a dramatic entrance…or at least the cake would have made a dramatic entrance…and I would have leapt out of it, like the Marilyn Monroe equivalent of a Jack in the Box, stunning you with my wonderful outfit. Then I would have sung you 'Happy Birthday', even though I'll be the first to admit that my voice is pretty average…'

'Unfortunately…' He edged away and looked at her with a shuttered expression. 'Unfortunately you couldn't have chosen a worse moment for your little surprise.'

'No, well…' Always so comfortable in his presence, Megan could feel stirrings of unease nibbling away inside her, even though really he no longer looked angry. 'You never told me that you were expecting guests. You said that you would be working, and I just thought that it would be kind of nice to be surprised. You work too hard.'

'I do what I have to do, Megan. How many times have I told you that?'

'Yes, I know. You hate this place, and you work hard so that you can get out of it and do something with your life.'

'I intend to do more than just *something* with my life.'

His father had done just *something* with his life. He had left poverty in Italy, hoping to find that the streets of London would be paved with gold. In the event they had been paved with tarmac and cement, just like everywhere else, and his father's talents, his tremendous mathematical brain which had so enchanted Alessandro as a young boy, had become lost in the mindless boredom of manual work—because he had not been qualified to do anything else, and provincial little England had not been kind to a man whose grasp of English was broken. Never mind that his wife was English. An English rose with as few qualifications as her Italian husband. An English rose whose hands had been prematurely old from the cleaning jobs she had held down so that they could afford a small holiday once a year by the cold British seaside.

Alessandro didn't like to think of the mother he had only known for the first ten years of his life. He liked even less to think of his father, loyally working for a haulage firm for twenty-five years, only to be made redundant at a time when he had been too old to get another job.

To his dying breath he had continued to tell his son what a wonderful life he had led.

To Alessandro's way of thinking his father's talents had been wasted, by lack of opportunity and the cruelty of a world that judged a man's worth by bits of paper. He would, he had determined from an early age, get those bits of paper, and he would control the world so that it could never control him the way it had his father.

'Those three men,' he said, keeping that unaccustomed drift of memory to himself, 'who were treated to your impromptu performance, are instrumental in my plan for the future.'

'You mean, the pinstriped crew?'

He paused. 'You need to grow up, Megan.'

That one statement, delivered with a coldness she had never heard before, was shocking. Yes, they were total opposites. They had laughed about that a million times. But he had always indulged her. She'd drag him away from his books with homemade picnics in the park and he would laugh at the sausage rolls and packets of biscuits and cheap wine. She would make a fool of herself singing karaoke, and he would shake his head in good-natured wonder and tell her never to consider a career in singing. He had never told her to grow up—and certainly never in that tone of voice.

'It was just meant to be a bit of fun, Alessandro. How was

I to know that the instruments of your plan would be here? And why do you have a plan, anyway? Really? Life's not a chessboard, you know.'

'That's exactly what it is, Megan. A chessboard. The life we end up getting depends entirely on the moves we make.'

'I know you want to do stuff with your life, Alessandro, but…' Megan shot him a look of bemusement. This wasn't quite the sort of talk she had been expecting, but it was certainly revealing. 'You can't plan *everything*. I mean, I really hope that I end up being a good teacher…'

'In a small country school somewhere…'

'What's wrong with that?'

'There's nothing wrong with it,' Alessandro told her patiently.

He looked at her expressive, open face and felt like a monster, but this was a conversation that had to be undertaken. His future had unexpectedly come rushing towards him like a freight train, leaving him no choice.

'Did you ever think about qualifying and going to teach somewhere else?'

'Somewhere else? Why should I? You know that St Nicks have offered me a post for after I qualify.'

Her face softened as she thought of the pleasing prospect of teaching the children there. She was nothing like the high-flier that Alessandro was, and her future might not be so ruthlessly controlled as his appeared to be, but it was still looking pretty rosy from where she was sitting.

'Where else should I be going to teach?'

'What about an inner-city school?'

'Why are we having this conversation? Is it because you're still mad at me—because I embarrassed you in front of those people? Don't be…You wait right here, and I'm going to get us both something to drink. Some wine…'

She didn't give him time to answer, or to follow up with

some more heavy-duty remarks about life choices. Instead, she stood up and did a little sexy shimmy, throwing him a seductive look over one shoulder, before heading for the kitchen and pouring them a large glass of wine each.

She'd kind of hoped that he would be undressed when she returned, because he was always, but *always*, predictable when it came to being turned on by her, but he wasn't. In fact, he was standing up, and he had an awkward look on his face that promised more *talking*.

Whatever those guys had said to him had obviously made him a little too thoughtful, and it was her duty, she told herself mischievously, to take his mind off matters. And at the back of her mind she knew she really didn't want to hear what Alessandro wanted to say….

A very good place to start would be with his shirt. She placed the glasses on the small, beaten-up round table by the window and pulled off the white shirt, which she casually tossed over a chair.

'Megan…' Alessandro turned away and leaned heavily against the wall. 'This isn't a good time for this.' He tensed as he heard her walk towards him. He could picture the teasing smile on her face.

'Don't tell me you're getting too old for sex,' she said to his averted back. 'You're only a year older!' She wrapped her arms around his torso and then slipped her hands under the tee shirt, gently rubbing his flattened brown nipples with the tips of her fingers.

Alessandro shuddered, furious with himself for not being able to push her away when he knew that he had to. For both their sakes.

He felt the push of her breasts against him and turned round with a stifled moan, his big body arching back in denial of the primitive instincts he seemed unable to control.

He closed his eyes and shuddered again.

Nine months of seeing her, practically living with her, even though her college was over twenty miles away. Out towards the country because, she had told him often enough, big cities gave her a headache. Something about her was irresistible.

She took his hand and guided it to the strap of the black swimsuit which she was still wearing.

'At least the cake wasn't real,' Megan murmured, already wet and hot for him. 'Can you imagine if I'd emerged covered in Victoria sponge?'

She stood on tiptoe so that she could kiss his neck, and even though he wasn't, as he usually was, devouring her with his hunger, he *was* responding. She could feel it in the tension of his muscles—and… She put her hand on him and shivered with pleasure at the very big, very hard indication of just how much he wanted her—even if, for some weird reason, he *was* trying to fight it.

'Mind you,' she said thoughtfully, 'you would have had to lick it all off…'

The image was too powerful for Alessandro. He looked at her, at the deep cleavage inviting him to touch, promising him physical satisfaction of the kind he had never known in his life before.

I am, he thought with a strange feeling of helplessness, *only a man, dammit*!

He hooked his fingers under the straps of the swimsuit and ran them up and down against her smooth skin.

'A man could lose himself in the thought of that,' he said roughly, and all thoughts of *talk* vanished as he pulled down the straps and gazed at her breasts, large in comparison to her small frame, and perfectly formed. Milky-white and succulently heavy, with rose-pink nipples like discs, pouting provocatively at him.

He pulled her shakily towards the sofa and then, kicking

off his shoes, lay down. He figured he had damn near found heaven as she moved on top of him, sitting just in the right spot, so that he could feel the friction of his hardness against her through his trousers. She leant forwards, letting her breasts dangle temptingly above his mouth, and with a groan of utter abandonment Alessandro took one of the proffered nipples into his mouth, losing himself in the sensation of tasting her. He suckled on it, then when he was finished lavished the same attention on the other.

He wanted her completely naked. With fierce, driven movements he rid her of the swimsuit, stopping her when she tried to pull the tee shirt over his head.

'But I want to see you...' Megan whimpered.

He didn't answer. Instead, he pushed her back, spreading her legs in one deft motion, and her protest died on her lips as she felt his tongue invade her, sliding and exploring her depths until she was squirming, turned on to the point where thinking became an impossibility.

'Alessandro!' She curled her fingers into his dark hair and tugged him up. She was breathing heavily, her eyes closed, and she felt him undo the zipper of his trousers so that he could free himself.

She wasn't even entirely sure that he had removed his trousers before driving deep into her, his thrusting urgent, taking her by surprise.

It was quick, fierce lovemaking, and afterwards they were both breathless and spent. Alessandro was unusually quiet as he pushed himself away from her, so that he could get back into his jeans and then fetch a bottle of water from the fridge, which he proceeded to drink in one long swallow.

'You need to get dressed, Megan, and then we'll talk.'

Megan felt a chill of fear race up and down her spine, obliterating everything in its path.

Talk about what? she was desperate to ask, but his shuttered expression kept that question reined in, and she silently went to the bedroom and rescued the only items of clothing she kept at his place: a pair of jeans and a sweater.

When she returned, it was to find that he had taken up position by the table, so that when she sat down, facing him, it felt like an awkward interview.

'If it's about my cake surprise, you have my word I won't do anything like that again. It'll take more than one shampoo before my hair recovers from the masking tape. In fact, I'm going to have to sack my production manager.'

Alessandro didn't return her grin. This was going to be a difficult conversation, made all the worse by the fact that they should never have made love. He had allowed himself a selfish luxury, one which he deeply regretted.

'This isn't about your cake surprise, Megan. This is about those three men who were here. I've been head-hunted.' It had come as no great surprise to Alessandro. He was good. He had been head-hunted before, and had turned down all offers. With or without intervention, he was going to go places—although this particular intervention would be helpful in the near future.

'Wow, Alessandro! That's fantastic! We should celebrate…' But it wasn't a celebrating atmosphere. 'You don't look overjoyed.'

Alessandro shrugged. 'Little do they realise it, but they will discover that they need me more than I need them.'

Megan laughed. 'Well, no one could ever accuse you of not having a healthy ego, Alessandro.'

That wonderful laugh stirred something inside him which he chose to ignore.

'I've been offered a job.' He stood up, distancing himself from her. 'In London.'

Those two words stilled the easy smile on her lips, replacing it with the cold hand of dread. 'London? But you can't go to London.' *What about us?* 'What about your Masters?'

'It will have to take a back seat. I can finish it in my own time, but for the moment my future calls.'

She was trembling. She had banked on having him around for a few more months, at which point she would be able to cross the inevitable bridge. That bridge was now staring her in the face. Maybe, she thought, desperately salvaging the best possible take on the situation, they could carry on a long-distance relationship? It wouldn't be ideal, but it could work. A few hours on the train every other weekend, and then there were the holidays…

'When?'

'Immediately.' Alessandro allowed the finality of that word to settle between them like a rock sinking into deep, uncharted waters. It hurt to look at her distraught expression.

'Immediately…as in *immediately*…?'

'Just time to pack up my belongings—what little I have—and put my past behind me for good.'

'It's not that bad,' she whispered. Thoughts and fears were whizzing around in her head and she was beginning to feel sick. 'What…what about us…?'

Alessandro didn't answer, and the silence stretched between them until she could almost hear it vibrating in the air.

'We…we can still carry on seeing each other, can't we? I mean, I know London's a long way away, but loads of people have long-distance relationships. It might be romantic! Who knows? We could…um…meet up every so often…' Her babbling trailed off into silence. More silence.

'It wouldn't work,' Alessandro said flatly.

'Why not? Wouldn't you even be willing to *give it a try*?' Desperation had crept into her voice, and she searched his face for the smallest sign of comfort. But she was looking at a stranger. His expression was closed and hard.

'There's no point, Megan.'

'No point? *No point?* How can you say that, Alessandro? We've practically *lived together* for the better part of a year! How can you say that there's *no point* in trying to stay together? I…we…Alessandro, *I love you.* I really do. You're the guy I gave myself to…you *know* how much that meant to me…'

Alessandro flushed darkly. 'And I cherish that gift.'

He said it as though their relationship had already been consigned to the memory box.

'Then tell me that you won't walk away.'

'I…I can't say that, Megan.' He embraced the room in one sweeping gesture with a look of distaste. 'This…this was a chapter in my life, Megan, and it's time for me to move on with the book.'

'What you're saying is that *I'm* a chapter in your life. You had your fun but all good things come to an end.'

'All things *do* come to an end. And your life is here, Megan. Here with your family, with your teaching job out in the country. You know you hate the city. You've always said that. You told me that the only reason you ever ventured into Edinburgh in the first place was because your cousin had dragged you there, and that the only reason you kept coming back was to see me… If you think Edinburgh's city living, then London is in a league of its own.'

'You're twisting everything I said to you! My life could be *anywhere* with you!'

'No.'

He almost wished that she would cry. A crying female he could deal with, because crying females had always irritated the hell out of him. But she wasn't a crier.

'You're a country girl at heart, Megan, and you would be

miserable if I—or anyone else, for that matter—removed you from the open fields you enjoy. That aside…' He paused, because he wanted to be completely honest with her. That much she deserved. 'This step of my journey I must take alone. I'm about to devote myself to my career. I literally wouldn't have time to spend…'

'…taking care of a hopeless country bumpkin like me?' Megan finished for him.

She stared down at her bare feet. The bright red nail polish she had applied to her toes earlier in the day was already beginning to flake. She would have to get rid of it. She actually hated bright red nail polish anyway. She had only put it on because it matched the Marilyn image she had wanted for her stupid, childish surprise cake gimmick.

'Taking care of *any woman*.' But maybe, he thought, there was some truth in her statement. Falling out of a box in front of three of the country's top finance gurus might seem a bit of a joke to her, but this was going to be his life, and falling out of boxes just wasn't going to cut it.

'I don't believe you.' Megan held her ground stubbornly, determined to wade through every inch of pain until the picture was totally clear in her head. 'You just don't think that I'm good enough for you now you're about to embark on this wonderful jet-setting career of yours. If I had been an… accountant, or…an economist, or someone *more serious*, then you wouldn't be standing there, airbrushing me out of your life as though I'd never existed!'

'What do you want me to say, Megan?' He finally snapped, furious that she was making this already difficult situation even more difficult by demanding answers to hypothetical speculations. 'That I can't see myself in a permanent situation with someone who will probably still be fooling around and singing karaoke when she's thirty-five?'

If he had extracted a whip from his back pocket and slashed it across her face it couldn't have hurt more, and she stared at him mutely.

'I apologise,' he said brusquely. 'That remark was entirely uncalled for. Why can't you just accept that there are limitations to this relationship and always have been?'

'You never mentioned anything about limitations before. You let me give you my undivided love and you never said a word about me not fitting the bill.'

'Nor did I ever speak to you about a future for us.'

'No,' Megan agreed quietly. 'No, you never did, did you?'

Alessandro steeled himself against the accusatory look in her big blue eyes. 'I assumed you were aware of the differences between us as well as I was—assumed you knew that my intention was never to remain in Scotland, playing happy families in a cottage somewhere in the middle of nowhere.'

'I assumed you cared about me.'

'We had fun, Megan.' He spun round and stared out of the grimy window to the uninspiring view two floors down. In the rapidly gathering dark the strip of shops opposite promised fish and chips, an all-you-can-eat Indian buffet every lunchtime, a newsagent and that was about it—because the other three shops were boarded up.

'Fun?'

Alessandro ignored the bitterness that had crept into her voice. When he had first made love to her, had discovered that she was a virgin, he had felt a twinge of discomfort. In retrospect, maybe he should have walked away at that point, rather than allowing her to invest everything into him, but he had been weak and—face it—unable to resist her. He was now paying the price for that weakness.

'You're better off without me,' he said roughly, as he continued to stare outside. 'You have all you need right here.

You'll teach at that school of yours, only a short distance away from all your family, and in due course you'll find a guy who will be content with the future you have mapped out.'

Megan had thought that the future she had mapped out for herself had *included him*!

'Yes,' she said dully. He wasn't even looking at her. He had already written her out of his life and was ready to move on. 'Why did you make love with me just now if you intended to get rid of me?' she asked. 'Was it a one-last-time session for poor old Megan before you sent her on her way?'

Alessandro spun round, but he didn't make a move towards her. 'It was…a…mistake…' And never again would he allow his emotions to control his behaviour.

He gripped the window sill against which he was leaning and reminded himself that, however much she was hurting now, she was still a kid and would bounce back in no time at all. She would even thank him eventually for walking away from her—would realise in time to come that they were worlds apart and whatever they had had would never have stayed the course of time. It was a reassuring thought.

Megan couldn't bear to look at him. She stood up, staring at the ground as though searching for divine inspiration.

'I think I'm going to leave now,' she said, addressing her feet. 'I'll just check the bedroom. See if there's anything of mine that I should take with me.'

He didn't try to stop her rooting through his stuff. The lack of anything belonging to her now seemed ominous proof of her impermanence in his life. He had never encouraged her to leave any of her things at his place. Sure, she's forgotten odd bits and pieces now and again, like the clothes she was currently standing in, but he'd always returned them.

The only things she had insisted on leaving were some of her CDs. She was voracious when it came to modern music, whereas he preferred more chilled sounds. *Easy listening to the point of coma*, she had teased him. Yet another example of those differences between them, which she had stupidly failed to spot but which he had probably noted and lodged away in his mind somewhere, to be brought out later and used in evidence against her.

Without looking in his direction, she quietly gathered her CDs and stuffed them in a plastic bag.

'I think that's about everything.' Some CDs, a toothbrush, some moisture cream, some underwear. Precious little. 'Good luck with the new job and the new life, Alessandro. I really hope it lives up to expectations and I'm sorry about the mess from the cake. You'll have to get rid of that yourself.'

Alessandro nodded. He didn't say anything because there was nothing left to say, and for the first time in his life he didn't trust himself to speak.

Megan turned away, and was half-disappointed, half-relieved when he didn't follow her. There was an emptiness growing inside her, and her throat felt horribly dry and tight, but there would be time enough to cry. Once she was back in her little room at college. Just one last look, though. Before she left for good. But when she turned around, it was to find that he was staring out of the window with his back to her.

CHAPTER ONE

MEGAN stooped down so that she was on the same level as the six-year-old, brown-haired, blue-eyed boy in front of her. Face of an angel, but spoiled rotten. She had seen many versions of this child over the past two years, since she had been working in London. It seemed to be particularly predominant at private schools, where children were lavished with all that money could buy but often starved of the things that money couldn't.

'Okay, Dominic. Here's the deal. The show's about to start, the mummies and daddies are all out there waiting, and the Nativity play just isn't going to be the same without you in it.'

'I don't want to be a tree! I hate the costume, Miss Reynolds, and if you force me then I'm going to tell my mummy, and you'll be in *big* trouble. My mummy's a lawyer, and she can put people into prison!' he ended, with folded arms and a note of irrefutable triumph in his voice.

Megan clung to her patience with immense difficulty. It had been a mad week. Getting six-year-old children to learn and memorise their lines had proved to be a Herculean feat, and the last thing she needed on the day before school broke up was a badly behaved brat refusing to be a tree.

'You're a very important tree,' she said gently. '*Very* important. The manger wouldn't be a manger without a very important tree next to it!' She looked at her watch and mentally tried to calculate how much time she had to convince this tree to take his leading role on stage—a role which involved nothing more strenuous than waving his arms and swaying. She had only been at this particular school for a term, but she had already sussed the difficult ones, and had cleverly steered them away from any roles that involved speech.

'I want my mummy. *She'll* tell you that I can be whatever I want to be! And I want to be *a donkey*.'

'Lucy's the donkey, darling.'

'I want to be a donkey!'

Tree; donkey; donkey; tree. Right now, Megan was heartily wishing that she had listened to her friend Charlotte, when she had decided to leave St Margaret's and opted for another private school. Somewhere a little more normal. She could deal with *normal* fractious children. She had spent three years dealing with them at St Nick's in Scotland, after she had qualified as a teacher. None of *them* had ever threatened her with prison.

'Okay. How about if we fetch your mummy and *she* can tell you how important it is for you to play your part? Remember, Dominic! It's all about teamwork and not letting other people down!'

'Donkey,' was his response to her bracing statement, and Megan sighed and looked across to where the head of the junior department was shaking her head sympathetically.

'Happened last year,' she confided, as Megan stood up. 'He's not one of our easier pupils, and fetching his mum is going to be tricky. I've had a look outside and there's no sign of her.' Jessica Ambles sighed.

'What about the father?'

'Divorced.'

'Poor kid,' Megan said sympathetically, and the other teacher grinned.

'You wouldn't be saying that if you had witnessed him throwing his egg at Ellie Maycock last Sports Day.'

'Final offer.' Megan stooped back down and held both Dominic's hands. 'You play the tree, and I'll ask your mummy if you can come and watch me play football over the vacation if you have time.'

Forty-five minutes later and she could say with utter conviction that she had won. Dominic Park had played a very convincing tree and had behaved immaculately. He had swayed to command, doing no damage whatsoever, either accidental or intentional, to the doll or the crib.

There was just the small matter of the promised football game, but she was pretty sure that Chelsea mummies, even the ones without daddies, were not going to be spending their Christmas vacation at home. Cold? Wet? Grey? Somehow she didn't think so.

Not that she had any problem with six-year-old Dominic watching her play football. She didn't. She just didn't see the point of extending herself beyond her normal working hours. She wasn't sure what exactly the school policy was on pupils watching their teachers play football, and she wasn't going to risk taking any chances. Not if she could help it. She was enjoying her job and she deserved to. Hadn't it taken her long enough to wake up in the morning and look forward to what the day ahead held in store for her?

From behind the curtain she could hear the sound of applause. Throughout the performance cameras and video recorders had been going mad. Absentee parents had shown up for the one day in the year they could spare for parental duty, and they were all determined to have some proof of their devotion.

Megan smiled to herself, knowing that she was being a little unfair, but teaching the children of the rich and famous took a little getting used to.

In a minute everyone would start filtering out of the hall, and she would do her duty and present a smiling face to the proud parents. To the very well-entertained parents—because, aside from the play, they would be treated to substantial snacks, including *crudités*, delicate salmon-wrapped filo pastries, miniature meatballs and sushi for the more discerning palate. Megan had gaped at the extravaganza of canapés. She still hadn't quite got to grips with cooking, and marvelled at anyone who could produce anything edible that actually resembled food.

Out of nowhere came the memory of Alessandro, of how he'd used to laugh at her attempts at cooking. When it came to recipe books she was, she had told him, severely dyslexic.

It was weird, but seven years down the road she still thought of him. Not in the obsessive, heartbroken, every-second-of-every-minute-of-every-waking-hour way that she once had, but randomly. Just little memories, leaping out at her from nowhere that would make her catch her breath until she blinked them away, and then things would return to normal.

'Duty calls!'

Megan snapped back to the present, to see Jessica Ambles grinning at her.

'All the parents are waiting outside for us to tell them what absolute darlings their poppets have been all term!'

'Most of them *have* been. Although I can think of a few…'

'With Dominic Park taking first prize in that category?'

Megan laughed. 'But at least he waved his arms tonight without knocking anyone over. Although I *did* notice that Lucy the donkey kept her distance. Amazing what a spot of blackmail can do. I told him he could watch my next football match.' She linked her arm through her colleague's and together they headed out to the main hall, leaving behind a backstage disaster zone of discarded props and costumes, all to be cleared away the following afternoon, when the school would be empty.

The main hall was a majestic space that was used for all the school's theatrical performances and for full assemblies. A magnificent Christmas tree, donated by one of the parents, stood in the corner, brightly lit with twinkling lights and festooned with decorations—many from the school reserves but a fair few also donated by parents. Elsewhere, along one side, were tables groaning with the delicacies and also bottles of wine—red and white.

The place was buzzing with parents and their offspring, who had changed back into their school gear, and numerous doting relatives. In between the teachers mingled, and enjoyed the thought that term was over and they would be having a three-week break from the little darlings.

Megan was not returning to Scotland for the holidays. Her parents had decided to take themselves off to the sunshine, and her sisters were vanishing to the in-laws'. Playing the abandonment card had been a source of great family mirth, but really she was quite pleased to be staying put in London. There was a lot going on, and Charlotte would be staying down as well. They had already put up their tree in the little house they shared in Shepherd's Bush, and had great plans for a Christmas lunch to which the dispossessed had been cordially invited. Provided they arrived bearing food or drink.

A surprising number of people had seemed happy to be included in the 'dispossessed' category, and so far the numbers were up to fifteen—which would be a logistical nightmare, because the sitting room was small—but a crush of bodies had never fazed Megan. The more the merrier, as far as she was concerned.

She heard Dominic before she actually spotted him. As was often the case with him, he was stridently informing one of his classmates what Father Christmas was bringing him. He seemed utterly convinced that the requested shed-load of presents would all be delivered, and Megan wondered whether he had threatened the poor guy with a prison sentence should his demands not be met.

She was smiling when she approached his mother, curious to see what she looked like. Matching parents to kids was an interesting game played by most teachers, and this time the mental picture connected perfectly with the real thing.

Dominic Park's mother *looked* like a lawyer. She was tall, even wearing smart, black patent leather flats, with a regal bearing. Dark hair was pulled back into an elegant chignon, and her blue eyes were clever and cool. Despite the informality of the occasion, she was wearing an immaculate dove-grey suit, with a pashmina loosely draped around her shoulders.

She was introduced via Dominic, who announced, without preamble, that this was Miss Reynolds and she had promised she would take him to watch her play football.

'You must be Dominic's mum.' Megan's smile was met with an expression that attempted to appear friendly and interested but somehow didn't quite manage to make it. This was a woman, Megan thought, who probably distributed her smiles like gold dust—or maybe she had forgotten how to smile at all, because it wasn't called for in a career that saw her putting people into prison, if her son was to be believed.

'Correct, Miss Reynolds, and I must say that I was very disappointed when Nanny told me today that Dominic would be playing a tree. Not terribly challenging, is it?'

She had an amazing accent that matched her regal bearing perfectly.

'We like to think of the Nativity Play as a fun production, Mrs

Park, rather than a competition.' She smiled down at Dominic, who was scowling at some sushi in a napkin. She took it from him. 'And you made a marvellous tree. Very convincing.'

'When will you be playing football?' he demanded.

'Ah… Timetable still to be set!'

'But you won't forget, will you?' he insisted. 'Because my mummy's a—'

'Yes, yes, yes… I think I've got the message on that one, Dominic.' Megan smiled at his mother. 'I've been told that I shall be flung into prison without a Get Out Of Jail Free card if I don't let him watch one of my matches….'

'Silly boy. I've told him a hundred times that I'm a corporate lawyer! And we shall have to discuss Dominic watching your football match, I'm afraid. We're very busy over the Christmas period, and Nanny won't be around for three days, so I shall be hard-pressed to spare the time to take him anywhere.'

Megan was busy feeling sorry for poor Nanny, who had clearly been inconsiderate enough to ask for time off over Christmas, when she was aware that they had been joined by someone. The elegant lawyer had stopped in mid-flow, and there actually was something of a smile on her face now as she looked past Megan to whoever was standing behind her.

'Alessandro, darling. So good of you. I'm absolutely *parched*.'

Alessandro!

The name alone was sufficient to send Megan into a tail-spin. Of course there was more than one Alessandro in the world! It was a common Italian name! It was just disconcerting to hear that name when she had been thinking about him only minutes earlier.

She turned around, and the unexpected rushed towards her like a freight train at full speed, taking her breath away. Because there he was. Alessandro Caretti. *Her* Alessandro.

Standing in front of her. A spectre from the past. Seven years separated memory from reality, but he had remained the same. Still lean, still muscular, still staggeringly good-looking. Yes, a little older now, and his face was harsher, more forbidding, but this was the man who had haunted her dreams for so long and still cropped up in her thoughts like a virus lying dormant in her bloodstream—controlled, but never really going away.

She had never seen him in a suit before. Seven years ago he had worn jeans and sweatshirts. He was wearing a suit now, a charcoal-grey suit, and, yes, a white shirt—so some things must not have changed.

Megan could feel the blood rushing into her face, and it was a job to keep steady, to hold out her hand politely and wonder if he would even recognise her. Her hair was shorter now, but still as uncontrollable as it always had been. Everything else was the same.

She was shaking when she felt the brief touch of his hand as she was introduced.

What was he doing here? Was he Dominic's *father*? But, no. From next to her she could hear that cut-glass accent saying something about her fiancé. He was engaged! Wearing a suit and engaged to the perfect woman he had foreseen all those years ago when he had broken up with her.

He didn't appear to recognise her as he held out the glass of wine to his fiancée, eliminating her from the scene by half turning his back on her.

On the verge of flight, she was stopped by Dominic announcing yet again—this time to Alessandro—that Miss Reynolds would be taking him to a football match. At this, Alessandro focused his fabulous dark eyes on her and said, unsmilingly, 'Isn't that beyond the call of duty, Miss Reynolds?'

How can you not even recognise me? Megan wanted to yell. Had she been so *forgettable*? Didn't he even recognise *her name*? Maybe he had met so many women over the years that faces and names had all become one great big blur.

'It seemed the only way to persuade Dominic to be a tree.' It was a miracle that her vocal cords managed to remain intact when everything else inside was going haywire. 'And it's not taking him to a football match. It would be to watch me playing football.'

'You play football?'

His dark, sexy voice wrapped itself around her, threatening to strangle her ability to breathe.

'One of my hobbies,' Megan said, taking one protective step back. She dragged her eyes away from that mesmerising face and addressed his fiancée. 'I hope you have a lovely Christmas, Mrs Park.' She realised that she was still clutching the discarded sushi, which had seeped through the napkin and was now gluey against the tightly closed palm of her hand.

'You'll have to give my mother your phone number, Miss Reynolds, and your address. For the football match? You promised!'

Two steps further back and a brief nod. 'Sure. I'll leave it on a piece of paper on the front desk. Now, I really must dash…meet some of the other parents… Very nice to meet you…'

Her eyes flickered across to Alessandro, then away. He wasn't even looking at her. He was sipping his wine, his eyes drifting in boredom across the room, indifferent to her babbling. An insignificant teacher. Why should he be interested in anything she had to say? He didn't even remember who she was!

For the next hour Megan kept her distance from them, but time and again she found herself seeking him out in the crowd. He was always easy to spot. He dominated the room—and not just with his powerful physical presence. He looked as though he owned the space around him and only the special chosen few were invited in.

She should really have stayed to the end, until after all the parents had departed, because a few of the teachers were planning on going out for a drink, but with her nervous system in total meltdown she fetched her coat, scribbled the wretched phone number and address on a piece of paper, which she left on the front desk, and headed for the underground.

It was a sturdy walk from the school, away from the chaos of expensive cars bearing the little darlings back home. After a few minutes there was only the sound of her boots on the pavement and the usual delightful London noises. The distant thrum of traffic, the occasional high-pitched whine of a police siren, the muted voices of people passing her.

Hunched into her coat and with her head down, braced against the freezing wind, Megan only became aware of the car after it had stopped right in front of her—and she only became aware of it then because she nearly crashed into the passenger door, which had been flung open.

Two words. 'Get in!'

Megan bent and peered into the car. She knew the driver of the car. Of course she did. She would have recognised that voice anywhere.

'Drop dead.' She slammed the door shut with such ferocity that she was surprised it didn't fall off its hinges.

The cool walk had restored some of her sanity, and she had figured out *why* he hadn't seen fit to say that they had met before. He was a successful city gent now, engaged to be married to his female counterpart. Why spoil the rosy picture by announcing any connection to a lowly teacher? Even *before* he had become successful—which he undoubtedly was, if the suit and the car were anything to go by—he had ditched her because she had been *inappropriate* to his long-term plans. How much more *inappropriate* would she be now?

The car cruised alongside her, its window now rolled down,

and she heard him say with lazy intent, 'You can either get in, or else I'll pay you a little visit at your house. Your choice.'

Megan looked through the window. 'What are you doing, Alessandro? I thought you didn't recognise me.'

'Naturally I recognised you. I just didn't see fit to launch into an explanation of how our paths had crossed. Wrong time, wrong place.'

The baldness of that statement only skimmed the surface of the shock he had felt on seeing her. To have your past leap out at you and grab you by the throat… He had felt driven to do this—to follow her on her way home—although now that he had Alessandro was beginning to wonder what would be achieved. Curiosity had got the better of him—maybe that had been it?

Somewhere in his seven-year meteoric rise to power, curiosity had become a rare luxury. His gift for money-making in the complex world of derivatives had engineered a swift rise to giddy, powerful heights. It had also provided him with more than sufficient disposable cash to move effortlessly into acquisitions. Alessandro had everything that money could buy, but the ease with which he had made millions had left him with a jaded palette. After his initial shock on seeing Megan, his curiosity to find out what she had been up to in the past seven years had been overpowering and irresistible, and—face it—he could indulge his curiosity. He could indulge anything he wanted to.

'What do you want?'

'Get in the car, Megan. It's been a long time. It would be bizarre not to play a little catch-up game, don't you think?'

'I think it's bizarre that you left your fiancée so that you could follow me.'

'Old friends meeting up. Victoria would have no problem with that. Thankfully she's not a possessive woman. I'll drop you home. It's a ridiculous night to be…doing what? Catching a bus? Taking a tube somewhere?'

'Go away.'

'Not still playing childish games, are you, Megan? You know you're as curious to find out about me as I am to find out about you, so why fight it?'

Megan got in. For one thing the wind was whipping her coat all over the place. For another the tube would be packed and uncomfortable, and quite possibly not running to schedule. And, yes, she *was* curious. He had been an important piece of her past, and maybe catching up, hearing all about his bright, shiny new life, would provide her with the tools for closure.

'Nice car.' She took in the walnut dashboard and the plush leather seats. 'I don't know much about cars, but I'm thinking that you climbed up that ladder without taking too many knocks on the way up, Alessandro.' She couldn't prevent the note of bitterness that had crept into her voice—a leftover from the hurt all that time ago.

'Did you ever think that I wouldn't?' He wasn't looking at her. His concentration was entirely on the road and on the illuminated map on his dashboard, detailing directions to her house. He had got the address from the scrap of paper she had left at the front desk, and had punched it into his navigation system as soon as he had got into his car, having safely seen Victoria and Dominic to a taxi.

Not looking at her, but still seeing her in his head, he thought she looked exactly as she had all those years ago. Curly blonde hair, big blue eyes, full mouth that always looked on the verge of laughing. He had had no choice but to follow her.

'Arrogance isn't a very nice trait.'

'Who's being arrogant? I'm being realistic. And *nice* isn't a trait that gets anyone very far in the business world. What are you doing in London, anyway?'

'Oh, I forgot. I was supposed to be a little country girl who was destined to stay in the country.'

'You're bitter.'

'Can you blame me?'

'I did what was necessary. For both of us. In life, we all do.'

His casual dismissal of her feelings was as hurtful as if he had taken a knife and twisted it into her. 'So…you live in London? Have you made a name for yourself? I know that was top of your list of things to do. Oh, along with making lots of money.'

'Yes, to your first question—and as far as making money, let's just say that I'm not living hand-to-mouth.'

'You mean, you're rich?'

'Filthy rich,' he agreed easily.

'You must feel very pleased with yourself that your plan worked out, Alessandro.' And the very suitable lawyer with her posh voice was obviously part two of his plan. He had dumped all handicaps and moved on, with the same relentless focus that she had seen in him years ago. 'And how did you meet…Dominic's mother?' she asked, twisting the knife herself now.

'Work,' Alessandro said abruptly.

'She tells me that she's a corporate lawyer.'

'The top of her field.'

'Guess she ticks all the boxes, then.' Megan thought of all the boxes *she* had failed to tick—but wasn't it stupid to still be bitter after all this time? He had moved on with his life and so, really, had she. Of course, he was getting married, which rated a lot higher on the *Moving On With Life* scale than having had a couple of boyfriends, neither of whom had lasted more than seven months, but she wasn't going to dwell on that.

'All the boxes,' Alessandro agreed smoothly.

'You've even managed to land yourself a ready-made family!'

'Dominic has his own father. I'm not required to play happy families with my fiancée's offspring.' In actual fact, Alessandro had met Dominic all of three times, even though he had now been seeing Victoria for six months. Their schedules were both ridiculously packed, and meetings had to be carefully orchestrated—usually dinner somewhere, or the theatre, or supper at his Kensington place. With his own personal chef, eating in was as convenient as dining out. Family outings, therefore, had not been on the agenda—something for which Alessandro was somewhat relieved.

'Charming,' Megan said brightly. 'I always thought that when you married someone you hitched up to *all* their baggage, including any offspring from a previous marriage. Crazy old me.'

'I don't remember you being sarcastic.'

'We're both older.' She shrugged and gave him the final directions to her house, which was only a few streets away. 'We've both changed. I don't remember *you* as being cold and arrogant.' Not that that didn't work for her. It did, because she disliked this new, rich Alessandro, with his perfect life and his ruthless face. 'You can drop me off here. It's been great catching up, and thanks for the lift.'

About to open the car door, she felt his hand circle her wrist. It was like being zapped by a powerful bolt of electricity.

'But we haven't finished catching up.' He killed the engine, but remained sitting in the dark car. 'You still have to tell me about yourself.'

Megan looked at him. 'Do you mind releasing me?'

'Why don't you invite me in for a cup of coffee?'

'I share a house. My housemate will be there.'

'Housemate?'

'Charlotte. Do you remember her, Alessandro? Or have

you wiped her out of your memory bank along with the rest of your past?'

'Of course I remember her,' Alessandro said irritably. Hell, here he was, being perfectly nice, perfectly interested, and what was he getting? She'd used to be so damned compliant, always smiling, always laughing, always keen to hear what he had to say, no sharp edges. 'And I have a very vivid recollection of my past. I just have no wish to revisit it.'

He had released her, but her whole body was still tingling from that brief physical contact.

'You can come in for a cup of coffee,' she told him. 'But I don't want you hanging around. You might think that it's all jolly good fun, taking a trip down memory lane, but—speaking as the person you dumped—I have zero interest in reliving old times.'

She opened the car door and walked towards the house, leaving him to decide what he wanted to do. She felt his presence behind her as she rustled in her bag for her keys, but she pointedly didn't look round at him as she slotted the key into the lock.

'The kitchen's through there,' she said, nodding towards the back of the house. 'I'm going to change.'

She took the stairs two at a time, her heart beating like a hammer. She couldn't believe that this was happening, that some quirk of fate had brought her past catapulting into her present. She also couldn't believe that seeing him could have such a huge impact on her. She had sometimes imagined what it would be like to see him again, never believing in a million years that it would actually happen. In her head she had been cool, contained, mildly interested in what he had to say, but with one eye on her watch—a busy young thing with a hectic life to lead, which didn't involve some guy who had dumped her because she didn't match up to the high standards he had wanted. In other words, a woman of twenty-six who was *totally over the creep*.

Now look at her! A nervous wreck.

She glanced at her reflection in the mirror and saw a flushed face and over-bright eyes. Charlotte, who would have given her a stiff pep talk on bastards and how they should be treated, was, of course, conspicuous by her absence. Where were friends when you needed them? Living it up with work colleagues somewhere in central London, instead of staying put just in case an urgent pep talk was required.

She was only marginally calmer when she headed downstairs fifteen minutes later, in a pair of faded jeans, an old sweatshirt, and her fluffy rabbit bedroom slippers—because, hey, why should she put herself out to dress up for a man whose taste now ran to sophisticated brunette lawyer-types with cut-glass accents?

He was waiting obediently in the kitchen, a graceful, powerful panther who seemed to dwarf the small confines of the room. He had removed his black coat, which lay over the back of one of the kitchen chairs, and was sitting at the table, his long legs extended to one side and elegantly crossed at the ankles.

'So…tell me what you've been up to these past few years,' he said, watching her as she turned her back on him to fill the kettle.

This, more than the woman in the black skirt and neat burgundy shirt, was the Megan he remembered. Casual in jeans and an oversized jumper and, as always when pottering inside her flat, wearing the most ridiculous bedroom slippers. Aside from kids, he'd always figured her to be the only person in the country who wore gimmicky bedroom slippers. His eyes drifted up her body, along her legs to her breasts, and he felt as though the room had suddenly become airless.

'I got my teacher training qualifications,' she said, stirring coffee into the boiling water and finally turning round to hand him a mug. 'Then I taught at St Nicks for three years. I moved down to London because Charlotte was working here and I thought it would make a change. I spent a year or so at St Margaret's, and I started working at Dominic's school in September.'

'That's a very dry, factual account. Why London? The last time I looked there were remarkably few open fields or running brooks, or little cottages with white picket fences.'

'I decided that I fancied a change from open fields, Alessandro. Maybe you were a little too quick to shove me into the role of the country bumpkin.' She wasn't going to tell him how claustrophobic her life had suddenly seemed the second he had walked out of it, how the excitement of teaching in a rural school had been tarnished with the uncomfortable feeling that outside her tiny world lay excitement and adventure. He didn't deserve to know anything about her.

'Look, I could embellish it with all the fun things I've done in between, Alessandro, but they would mean nothing to you.'

'Try me.'

'I'd rather not. I'm tired, and I don't have the energy.' Acutely conscious of those dark, fabulous, watchful eyes on her face, Megan took a sip of coffee and stared down at the table.

'I see you're still buying those ridiculous bedroom slippers.'

'Christmas present last year from one of my pupils,' she said crisply, tucking her feet beneath the table. 'It's one of the perks of the job. Lots of bath stuff, candles, picture frames and, in this case, gimmicky slippers.'

'How long have you lived here?'

'Since I moved to London.'

'Is this going to be a question and answer session?' Alessandro drawled. 'I ask the questions and you use as few words as humanly possible to answer?'

'You wanted to find out what I'd been up to and I'm tell-ing you. My life is probably not nearly as fascinating as yours has been, but I love what I do and I'm very happy.' She drained her cup, then looked at him. 'How long have you known… Dominic's mum?'

'Roughly six months.'

Roughly six months! Less time than he'd been with *her*. It hurt to think that he must have been bowled over to have moved from dating to engagement in such a brief period of time.

'Not long. A whirlwind romance?' She forced a smile. 'It must be the icing on the cake, Alessandro. I'm very happy for you.'

Alessandro hadn't thought about it as a *whirlwind ro-mance*. He had met Victoria when she had been working with her firm of lawyers on one of his deals. He'd liked her, ad-mired her intelligence, and appreciated her ability to respect his ferocious working agenda. Was that *romance*? It had cer-tainly been enough for him to take the next step forward, but he had to admit that it was at least partly fuelled by the fact that he wasn't getting any younger.

Unlike a lot of his city colleagues—men in their thirties, climbing the ladder to success—Alessandro had no intention of remaining a bachelor because of a preference for playing the field. Nor was he going to hang around until he was too old to enjoy playing with his kids. Sure, he had had women, but some restless, dissatisfied urge had always held him back from commitment.

Victoria, he recognised, was undemanding. She had her own high-powered job, and therefore did not look to him for constant companionship. Nor did she nag for assurances about love or any such thing. She worked for him and he, he sus-pected, worked for her. It was a mutually gratifying situation.

'Icing on the cake?' he mused. 'Yes, I suppose it is….'

CHAPTER TWO

IT HAD not been a satisfying meeting with Megan.

Alessandro stared out of his floor-to-ceiling office window at the busy, grey London streets five storeys below. Wet pavements were illuminated by lights, and everyone seemed to be laden down with shopping. The usual splurge of money-spending on presents—at least half of which would inevitably be returned to the shops on the first working day after Christmas because they didn't fit the bill. He had already bought something for Victoria—a diamond necklace which had cost the earth and which he had dispatched his personal assistant to source with the guiding words that it should be classy and very expensive. His personal assistant was extremely efficient.

Thinking about Christmas presents made him think about the one and only Christmas present he had ever bought for Megan. A pair of tickets for a concert by a band she had been crazy about. A dark, intimate venue where the noise had made the walls vibrate. They hadn't been able to stop grinning.

The memory surfaced seemingly from nowhere, and Alessandro frowned and thought back to his unsatisfactory meeting with Megan. He didn't know what he had been expecting, but the conversation had been awkward, forced, and the more awkward and forced it had become, the keener he had been to go beyond her polite responses and get the real flavour of the person sitting so stiffly opposite him.

He had left the house forty-five minutes after he had arrived, with the very clear impression that he had only been invited for a cup of coffee because she had found herself between a rock and a hard place, and that, having invited him in, she had been utterly uninterested in talking to him. Every word had been squeezed out of her, and each word had been less informative than the one before.

The woman hated him and couldn't be bothered to hide the fact.

Having enemies was part and parcel of Alessandro's life. Every successful man had his fair share. But his enemies would never have dared show their faces—and he had never known any woman to be less than madly in love with him! He knew that Megan had good reason. Just as he knew that breaking up with her at the time had been for her own good, whether she accepted that fact or not. There had been an innocence about her approach to life that would have been damaged had he dragged her along in his wake. He had made an attempt to tell her that, but she had listened to him politely, head cocked to one side, and then had said in a cool little voice, 'Whatever.'

Nor had he been able to get her to talk about her private life. Was she seeing someone? He couldn't imagine Megan making such a long-haul transfer, leaving behind her family, unless a man was involved. But when he had asked—out of *genuine interest*—all he had got was the same polite smile and, 'That's really none of your business, is it, Alessandro?'

Victoria's call interrupted his frowning contemplation telling him that she and Dominic were in Reception.

Family outing number one—and Alessandro hadn't objected because the outing in question was to the promised football game, which Dominic had followed up on with unexpected tenacity for a six-year-old kid. Football games didn't usually feature high on Dominic's agenda. His father lived in New York and only assumed a parental role once a year, for a fortnight when he came to London. And Alessandro certainly couldn't see Victoria slashing her work commitments to take him to a football match, or even for that matter, arranging football lessons for him. She wouldn't be able to commit to picking him up from them.

The vague feeling of dissatisfaction that had sat on his shoulders ever since he had bumped into Megan three days previously was dispelled slightly by a mental tallying of all the things he had in common with his fiancée—first and foremost their overriding work ethic.

It was all well and good for Megan to sit there with icy hostility stamped all over her face, as though he had single-handedly been responsible for coining the word *bastard*. What she didn't realise was that long-term relationships were built on more than just fun and romance. In fact, when it came to marriage, it was far more likely to succeed as a business proposition.

It frustrated him that he hadn't been able to convey that message to her three days ago. He might not now be scowling as he slung on his coat and headed for the elevator had he done so.

No one enjoyed being vilified for a crime they hadn't committed, and Alessandro was no exception.

In fact, he decided, as the elevator doors pinged open and he spotted Victoria and her son sitting on the low olive-green and chrome sofa in the reception area, it was almost a *good* thing that he would be seeing Megan again. If he had a chance to have a word with her—he certainly wouldn't be *engineer-*

ing any such thing, but if the situation arose—then he would tell her, politely but firmly, that they had both been kids when they had broken up. That it had been for the best. That it was ridiculous for her to be carrying a grudge after seven years.

He was barely aware of Dominic fidgeting next to him in the back seat of his Bentley, which his chauffeur was driving, and he only vaguely tuned in and out of Victoria's conversation—which he would have to get back to later, because it involved an offshore deal he was working on at the moment.

In fact, he was finding that he was actively anticipating seeing Megan's face when she realised that he had shown up to her football game. Trust Megan to have a hobby most normal women would steer clear of. He tried to picture Victoria in a football kit, running around on a field somewhere, but his imagination couldn't stretch to it. She was impeccably well bred, impeccably dressed and utterly uninterested in sport—both playing and watching.

He reached behind Dominic and absent-mindedly caressed her neck, just as the car pulled up to the school grounds.

Caught up in a tackle, Megan briefly registered Dominic's arrival before refocusing on the game.

She had known he would be coming because his mother had got her secretary to call her. She assumed the unfortunate nanny had been manoeuvred into this particular duty, and then forgot all about it for the remainder of the game—which was a very muddy, very physical, very invigorating one.

An hour later she walked across to three people barely visible because it was now so dark. She would have a two-minute chat with Dominic and maybe try and interest him in some football lessons—a plan which she had already mentioned to Robbie, the guy who coached at the school. In fact, coached at various schools.

'You tell me his mother's a hard-nosed lawyer?' Robbie had slung his arm around her shoulder. 'Just my type. Sure I'll take the kid on.'

'A hard-nosed *engaged* lawyer.' Megan had laughed. 'Who won't be at the match anyway. Just try and get Dominic interested in some lessons. I think it would do him good.'

An absentee father who lived in New York, as she had discovered from Jessica at school, and a soon-to-be stepfather who didn't see parenting someone else's child as part of his job description. It was a lose-lose situation for the poor kid, and a little outdoor fun wouldn't hurt him.

She was trying to untangle her hair from the elastic band which had started off the evening in place but seemed to have travelled in the wrong direction during the game, when she looked at bit more carefully at the three figures taking shape in front of her.

There was Dominic in the middle, huddled in a dark coat, and on either side of him…

Megan felt the colour surge into her face. His mother—surprisingly—and Alessandro.

She had thought to have seen the last of him after their horrible little *catch-up chat*, which had been more painful for her than Chinese water torture. Seeing him again out of the blue had stirred up a hornets' nest in her head. Now here he was, larger than life and playing happy families.

'You scored a goal, Miss Reynolds! And you're covered in mud!' Dominic sounded delighted at this revelation.

'If you're not careful, I shall put some on you!' She was caked in mud from head to foot, while Alessandro stood there watching her in his city suit and his beautiful coat and his very, *very* clean handmade Italian leather shoes. And Dominic's mother looked even more impeccable. How on earth could anyone watch a football match in high-heeled shoes?

'Dominic has had a super time. Thank you so much for asking him along to watch you, Miss Reynolds.'

'No problem.' She made sure not to look at Alessandro. 'I…er…I actually wanted to talk to you about maybe letting Dominic have football lessons, Mrs Park…'

'I'm afraid that's quite out of the question, Miss Reynolds.'

She hadn't finished the sentence before Dominic was jumping up and down in a state of high excitement.

'He might take you to court if you don't agree,' Megan said lightly, and the other woman managed to crack a smile at that. Depressingly, Megan found that it was hard to dislike her, because somewhere under that hard-edged, business-like surface she sensed a nice person.

'I'll leave you to think about it, anyway. I'm going to make my escape and get cleaned up. Have a brilliant Christmas!'

She still hadn't looked in Alessandro's direction, but she could feel his eyes on her. Even more depressing than the fact that she couldn't hate his fiancée was the fact that she was still mortifyingly aware of *him*. Two miserable seconds in his company and he was back in her thoughts as though it was yesterday.

She fled towards the changing rooms—angry with him for rubbing his jolly, settled, oh-I've-found-the-perfect-woman life in her face, and angry with herself because he still got to her and it wasn't fair.

She was flinging all her dirty kit into her bag when something made her look up—to find the object of her thoughts lounging by the door to the changing room, arms folded, watching her.

'What are you doing here? This is the women's changing room, in case you hadn't noticed!'

'The only woman in here is you. I waited outside, expecting to see you emerge with the rest of them, but after fifteen minutes I thought I'd come in. Make sure you hadn't collapsed.'

'Well, I haven't, so you can leave now.' She had showered, washed her hair and blowdried it, and put it into two stubby plaits. She had changed into jeans and a jumper and her thick waterproof anorak, which was a fashion disaster but could withstand anything the weather could throw at it.

'You played a good game out there. Football. Hmm… Wonder why I'm not surprised?' Covered in patches of mud, she had looked like an urchin. A very cute, very willful little urchin.

'What are you still doing here, Alessandro?' She snatched up her kit bag and drew in a deep breath before walking to the door. 'I haven't collapsed, and your fiancée will be waiting outside for you.'

'Victoria's been swept off her feet by your coach chap, who's taken her and Dominic to some coffee bar round the corner to discuss football lessons.'

'Robbie?' Megan paused, and then burst out laughing.

'What's so funny?' Alessandro said with a tight smile, feeling as though he was standing on the edge of some private inner joke. Did she laugh that laugh with *him*, the blond, athletic football coach who had managed to persuade Victoria out of her tightly allotted timetable?

'You wouldn't get it.' Megan brushed past him, still amused at her rogue of a coach, who had obviously charmed the very proper Mrs Park into breaking with tradition and taking time out.

'I haven't lost my sense of humour,' Alessandro told her with irritation.

'I'm sorry,' Megan apologised insincerely. 'Is that what you thought? No, I was just thinking about Robbie, that's all. He always manages to put a smile on my face.'

'Does he, now?'

'I'm not sure where *you're* going, but I'm heading for the bus stop. You're more than welcome to stand in the biting cold and wait with me, but I don't suppose you do public transport these days?'

'Give me five minutes.'

'Give you five minutes to do *what*?'

'To explain to Victoria that I'm going to see you home, and to tell my driver to wait for both of them.'

'No!' Megan stood with her hands on her hips, her football kit dumped on the ground next to her. 'This isn't going to do, Alessandro.'

Her heart was thumping inside her. He was so tall, so dominant, and her head was so full of memories that made her weak and vulnerable. But she was going to stand her ground—because what gave him the right to swan into her life after seven years and turn it upside down?

'We've had our little chat. I don't know how much clearer I can be when I tell you that I don't want you in my life. I made a fool of myself over you seven years ago, but I'm a different person now. We have nothing in common and nothing to talk about! You're not my friend, and quite honestly…' she crossed her fingers behind her back '…I have no idea what I ever saw in you in the first place.'

'Don't you? Well, the sex was pretty good.'

Megan flinched as though she had been struck, and Alessandro raked restless, frustrated fingers through his hair. He hadn't intended to say that. In fact, even harking back to the sex they had had made him feel as though he had crashed through an invisible barrier that should have remained intact.

'Forget I said that. Like everything else between us, that is history. I'm here because I didn't like the way things were left between us.'

'Not my problem.'

She began walking towards the bus stop—sports bag in one hand, rucksack slung over one shoulder, and yet another bag, over the other shoulder. She felt him take the sports bag out of her hand and she spun round, glaring.

'What do you think you're doing?'

'Don't you want to go and see what your boyfriend is up to?' He dangled the bag over his head and watched as she simmered impotently in front of him. God knew, but hearing her say that she regretted ever going out with him had touched a raw nerve— and who the hell was this Robbie character to her, anyway?

Momentarily distracted by his misconception that Robbie was her boyfriend, Megan laughed again—that rich, warm laugh that could still find some crazy crack in his armour that he hadn't been aware even existed.

'Maybe I should…' She trailed the words out, as if giving them a lot of thought. 'Do you think he might need protecting from your fiancée?'

'You really *have* changed, Megan. I remember when we used to go out you couldn't even tolerate the thought of me *looking* at another woman, never mind having a cup of coffee with one.'

'Yes, I remember. It was a very unhealthy place to be, had I but known it at the time.' Why did this feel so dangerous? she wondered. How could these unpleasant, unproductive exchanges make the hairs at the back of her neck stand on end and give her the giddy sensation that she was walking a tightrope?

'Maybe I *will* go and see what Robbie's up to,' she said, just in case he really did decide to get on the bus with her. 'Although I think you should be the one to worry. Little tip here, Alessandro. Robbie could charm the birds from the trees if he put his mind to it. And, since you're so intent on playing the gentleman that you're not…' she dumped all her bags at his feet '…you can carry the lot.'

She eased her tired shoulders and looked at him, wondering if he would reconsider his decision to hound her and tell her to carry her own bags. He didn't. He effortlessly picked up all her bags, and seemed to have little concern for the welfare of his expensive clothes.

'So you think I should be worried about your football coach, do you?' Alessandro's voice was threaded with amusement.

'It's not all about money,' Megan snapped, walking towards the only coffee shop in the vicinity—the same one they all used after football games.

'Do you really think that Victoria is interested in my money? More to the point, do you really think that *I* would give the time of day to *any* woman if I thought she *was* after my money?' He laughed shortly. 'Victoria wouldn't look twice at a man who wasn't as driven as she is.'

'What an exciting life the two of you must lead. Do you spend hours talking about work, and how wonderful it is that neither of you has any fun?'

'Whoever said that we don't have fun, Megan?'

That low, silky voice sent a nervous tremor rippling through her—made her think about all the things he and his fiancée might do for fun. She thought about him sharing his nights with the other woman, waking up to her, congratulating himself on the perfect match they made.

'I can't say that I'm interested one way or the other, actually.'

'No, you made that perfectly clear the last time I tried to engage you in conversation.'

'Which reminds me—have you told Dominic's mother that we know one another?'

'Naturally.' Alessandro shrugged. As he had predicted, Victoria had been surprised, but not alarmed.

'And she didn't mind?'

'That I dropped you home? Why should she? It's hardly as though there's anything between us now.'

He thought of her in her jeans and jumper, wearing her ridiculous slippers which he imagined had been some kind of protest vote at him being under her roof. She hadn't been wearing a bra, and he didn't know how he had known that. Maybe the swing of her full breasts under the cloth as she had reached over to hand him his mug of coffee, or maybe he just *knew*, because her body had once been his and the familiarity of a woman you possessed never quite left you.

'She has her own ex-boyfriends,' Alessandro commented neutrally. 'In fact, she regularly sees one of them—an investment banker who works in the city. It's no big deal.'

'I can't believe you're so…*civilised*…about your fiancée having a relationship with an ex, Alessandro. My, my, my…what's happened to all that Italian possessiveness? *I* may have been jealous, but let's not forget that *you* blew a fuse every time you saw me talking to one of my male friends from university.'

'Like you said, Megan, an unhealthy place. How long have you known this football-coach character, anyway? Was he the reason you decided to move down to London? I suspected that a man must have been involved.'

'I would never let a man influence any of my decisions,' Megan told him scornfully. If he wanted to think that she and Robbie were involved, then why not let him? 'I met Robbie after I came to London and he's a great guy.'

'A football coach?'

'He's more than just a football coach, Alessandro, and there's no need to play the snob card. You weren't always rich—in case you had forgotten!'

'Ah, but I always knew I would be. There's a difference between a man with ambition and a man who enjoys doing nothing with his life. Here's a piece of advice for you, Megan—your football coach will age into an overweight ex-athlete; ask yourself whether you'll find his lack of drive such a bundle of laughs then. Are you going to be happy serving him up his food on a tray in front of the television in the two-bedroom house you've stretched yourselves to buy? With a couple of kids squawking in the background?'

Alessandro didn't know why he felt compelled to pour cold water on her relationship. He supposed that it sprang from the remnants of the feelings he'd once had for her, and a certain amount of guilty awareness that he had been, just maybe, a little harsh when he had dispatched her.

She didn't answer, and her lack of response was like a red rag to a bull.

Couldn't the woman see that he was being *kind* in pointing out the obvious?

'What I choose to do with my life isn't your concern, Alessandro. There's the café. I can't believe Robbie managed to persuade your fiancée to have a coffee in a place that serves bacon and eggs all day to lorry drivers and cabbies.'

Ahead of them, the café was bursting at the rafters. Once upon a time this would have been the kind of crowd he regularly mingled with, sitting in some half-baked café, ploughing into a bargain fry-up. Outside, a group of youths were larking around, wearing hoodies. It was like looking through a glass window at his past, and for a few mad seconds Alessandro felt the kick of nostalgia. He reached out and yanked Megan back.

'The guy's a loser,' he said abruptly. 'And I'm telling you this for your own good, Megan.'

'You've never done anything *for my own good*, Alessandro!'

'You wouldn't last a minute with the kind of people I mix with.'

'Would that be because I'm a loser as well?'

'Dammit!' He released her and raked frustrated fingers

through his hair. He would have to stop doing this—touching her. 'You know what I'm saying!'

'Yes. I know you're insulting me.'

They looked at each other, their eyes tangling in the darkness, and Alessandro drew his breath in sharply. Those lips—he wanted to crush their softness under his, wanted to sweep his hands under her jumper and lose himself in her glorious body. He pulled back, breathing thickly.

'Not that it's any of your business, but Robbie only does football coaching on the side! He's studying for a law degree.'

Alessandro found that he preferred to think of the man as a loser. 'Bit old for that, wouldn't you say?'

'Not everyone knows what they want to be from the age of ten! Robbie knows what he wants to be now, and he's working bloody hard to get there! He's going to get his law qualifications and work to help the little people. Those people who don't have a voice, because they don't have loads of money to employ lawyers who charge the earth.'

'A do-gooder, in other words…' His voice was laced with disdain, but he was sickeningly aware that that was just the sort of guy Megan *would* lose her head over.

'Call it what you like.'

'Are you in love with him?'

Megan didn't answer that. Telling an outright lie was beyond her. She was deeply fond of Robbie, and admired his drive and his idealism, but they had never had that kind of relationship. And who the hell was Alessandro to even *ask* her that question? Did he think that he had a right to *feel sorry for her*? Because he had moved on? Found everything that he had been looking for? The right life with the right woman?

'I really hope Robbie's managed to convince your fiancée that Dominic should do some football out of school. Don't you?' Her voice was cool and tight. 'It must be hard for him.

I think that boys need a father figure—a role model they can look up to.'

'Is that some kind of veiled criticism?'

Because he had moved beyond criticism. That had been a lifetime ago, if it had ever existed at all. Now he occupied that sacred realm of men who were surrounded by sycophants, telling them everything they wanted to hear. He had buried the demons of his past and created a life of unsurpassed ease—a life he controlled. He had become untouchable. If only his parents could see him now—could see what riches could be born out of hardship.

'No, it's not. Dominic is a superbright boy, but being superbright can be as much a curse as a blessing. He's prone to boredom, and boredom makes him destructive. Football would enable him to expend all his energy.'

'And your boyfriend's just the guy to help him do that?'

'Stop calling him my *boyfriend*!'

'Okay, then. What about *lover*?'

'To answer your question—yes, Robbie would be just the guy to take Dominic in hand. He's great with kids.'

As far as answers went, that wasn't what Alessandro had been looking for, but they were already entering the café, and continuing the conversation was impossible.

There was a smile on Megan's face as she spotted the three of them sitting at the far end—two in front of mugs of coffee and Dominic with his chin cupped in his hand, staring in fascination at the blond-haired, blue-eyed do-gooder, who was smiling and talking with a lot of hand gestures and body language.

Just her type, Alessandro thought dismissively. She had said that he could charm the birds from the trees, and Victoria certainly seemed to be in a good mood, cutting an elegant figure among the crowd in the café like a…like a…

He couldn't help it. His eyes were drawn to the small blonde with her back to him as she strolled across to her boyfriend, who was now grinning at her.

Like a rose among thorns, he thought, hastily refocusing on Victoria.

'Have you been sold on the football lessons?' he asked, breaking up the trio at the table as he walked across.

'All sorted.'

Mother and son smiled at one another. Alessandro hadn't been around the two of them together much, but he was sensing that this was something of a rare occurrence, and he forced himself to smile at the man who was now standing up, reaching out with an open, good-natured expression, asking him if he wanted anything to eat and then joking about the quality of the coffee while telling him that the egg and chips were second to none.

He was ruffling Megan's pigtails, yanking them playfully, abstractedly, as though the gesture was a familiar one.

And Dominic was still staring at him, his mouth half open and his eyes wide.

From ruffling Megan's hair, he moved to ruffle Dominic's.

'So,' he said, still grinning, 'it's a date, then, is it? You? Me? The next Chelsea football match?' He turned to Victoria, now rising to her feet too, after, it would seem, eating *egg and chips*. 'You'll have to come too, of course. All of us should go together—have a bit of an evening out!'

Frankly, Alessandro couldn't think of anything worse, but he was very much aware that the loser was drawing Megan against him, and that both of them were laughing and saying something about the Chelsea football team. He wasn't sure what.

'See you before then, anyway!'

'How's that?' Alessandro looked at Robbie with a cool frown. 'Christmas? Christmas Day?'

'What are you talking about, Robbie?' Megan asked. She was thrilled to see her little tyrannical pupil hanging on to every word Robbie was saying. She suspected that a humble football might well be finding its way to his Christmas list, as a last-minute request.

'Hope you don't mind...' Robbie gave her waist an affectionate little squeeze, and Megan just *knew* that she wasn't going to like what was coming next. 'I've asked this disreputable rabble to come along on Christmas morning for a drink, if they're not doing anything special!'

'Come along *for a drink*?'

'You know our dispossessed little crowd...!' He winked at Dominic's mother. 'Nanny, I gather, is missing in action on Christmas Day...tut, tut, tut...and so Vicky here has pretty much promised that she would like nothing better than to fling a turkey in the oven and head to where it's all happening! *Your* house!'

'But...' Megan smiled apologetically, and swore to herself that she would do untold damage to Robbie just as soon as they were in private somewhere.

'Of course.' Alessandro looked at her, one hand in his trouser pocket, the other slung round his fiancée's shoulder. 'Why not?' He kissed Victoria on her temple. 'What do you say? My chef is on duty twenty-four-seven. He can get our lunch prepared and we can head to...*where it's all happening*...'

'It's a very small house...!' Megan glanced at Dominic, because the one thing kids hated was to be confronted by their teachers out of school hours. Unfortunately he didn't appear to be conforming to the stereotype. 'It'll be very crowded...' she stammered. 'You wouldn't believe the amount of people who seem to have nothing going on on Christmas Day... I'm sure you'll be all wrapped up with... opening presents...and stuff...'

'Of course we wouldn't dream of intruding,' Dominic's mother said, her exquisite good manners coming to the fore.

Megan smiled weakly. 'No—you wouldn't be, Mrs Park. It's open house…as Robbie said…just drop in, if and when you get the chance!'

'And please do stop calling me *Mrs Park*…' This time the smile was real, and it didn't look as though it had required lots of effort. 'I realise that it's not exactly protocol, but do call me Victoria.'

'Victoria…right…'

What a tableau they must make. She, Robbie, a kid who seemed to be undergoing a severe case of sudden hero-worship syndrome, and a man and a woman who might have stepped straight out of the pages of a magazine—although she was slightly gratified to notice that Alessandro's pristine suit was no longer in quite the same condition as it had been an hour before.

'And of course I'm Megan.' She winked at Dominic, and tried a friendly, teacher-like chuckle, but he was still staring at Robbie. There was ketchup smeared round his mouth and he was clutching a chip as though it was a once-a-year treat that might just vanish at any moment. 'And, yes…please… feel free to join us on Christmas Day!' Her laugh sounded a tad hysterical. 'The more the merrier!'

CHAPTER THREE

THINGS were under control. In support of the three vegetarian guests coming, and in frank and open acknowledgement of the fact that neither she nor Charlotte were any good in the kitchen—particularly when the meal involved handling raw meat—turkey was off the menu. Instead they had gone for loads of salads and a poached salmon, which their local fish-monger had kindly supplied, cut-rate, for his two pretty customers. In return they had given him a Christmas present of a ceramic vase—made by Charlotte, materials provided by Megan—which he solemnly promised would take pride of place on his mantelpiece.

Drinks were in liberal supply. Homemade punch, which was lethally strong, several bottles of wine, and some beer for the guys.

It had left a satisfying amount of time for Megan to take her time getting ready, and she was going all out. They had decided on a colour theme for the guests. Green and red. Christmas colours. Accordingly, Megan had found the perfect red dress. It clung like a second skin to mid-thigh, and was offset by some lacy tights in an interesting shade of bright green. Megan was pretty sure she looked like a deranged elf, but nevertheless she was pretty pleased with the result.

Being a teacher was in danger of turning her into a conformist. She felt that she should be allowed to be ridiculous for one day in the year.

Some might say that the red hair was taking things a bit too far, but it was a wash-in, wash-out colour, so that was all right.

She looked critically at her reflection in the mirror, not sure whether red hair really suited her, but it made a change from being blonde. Made her look wild. Especially with the cling-film dress, the fluorescent tights and the fabulous red shoes. She was sure she would never be able to walk properly in them.

It had turned out in the end that Alessandro and entourage *weren't* coming. Robbie, who seemed to have developed a cordial relationship with Victoria over the very short space of a week, had reliably informed Megan that she would be too busy in the morning, doing 'Christmas stuff'.

'Fiancé's chef will need some supervision,' he had said, shaking his head. 'No nanny and a chef unfamiliar with the territory. Never let it be said that life in the fast lane can't be tough.'

'I know,' Megan had replied, relieved that she wouldn't have to face the ordeal of feeling persecuted in her own house on the one day when she was owed relaxation. 'Much easier to just scrap the Christmas meal altogether and head for the salad counter. Somewhere in the country there'll be a turkey thanking us.'

She was feeling very relaxed as she put the finishing touches to her outfit. Some bright red lipstick and matching nail polish. On her bed was an assortment of Christmas presents. From her parents, much-needed cash and a necklace. From her sisters, clothes and make-up, and a very jolly Christmas card that cracked a supercorny joke when opened. From her friends, presents largely of the ridiculous nature. Right now she was wearing some earrings in the shape of Christmas trees. Fabulous.

And she wasn't going to think about Alessandro at all today. She had spent way too much time thinking about him, ever since he had resurfaced in her life like a bad dream she'd thought she had finally put to rest. Today she was going to relax and have fun.

An hour later and the punch was helping with her mission. She and Charlotte had put it together, making up the recipe as they went along. They hadn't been entirely sure of the ingredients, but had figured that, if in doubt, better too much alcohol than too little. It was consequently very potent and now almost finished, thanks to a houseful of nearly twenty people, all of whom had come bearing an interesting array of food. The kitchen table and counters were groaning under the weight of a nut loaf, a lentil loaf, several quiches, cold ham, sausages, and salads of every description. There was even a huge pot of curried chicken, courtesy of Amrita, one of Charlotte's friends from work.

Somewhere along the line someone had stuck a silver cardboard crown on Megan's head, which was tilting precariously to one side. The music was blaring and there was Robbie, more sober than might have been expected, taking on the role of host. He was decked out in a pair of red surfer shorts—the only red item of clothing he'd been able to rustle up from his wardrobe, he had told them—and an outrageously green shirt which he had bought from a charity shop especially for the occasion. Megan had to admit that he looked pretty good, with his blonde hair and blue eyes and muscular body. She grinned and waved, and he weaved over towards her.

'Your crown's slipping,' he said, righting it and then standing back to inspect his handiwork. 'You're in danger of your people revolting if they think you're no longer in charge of the throne, Your Majesty.'

Megan had to smile. 'You seem to have been getting along

like a house on fire with Dominic's mum,' she remarked. She had been meaning to prise a few more details about *that* from him, and had had no chance thus far.

'She's a very nice lady,' he said, before waxing lyrical about the importance of sport for young kids and Dominic's enthusiasm to join a football club.

'You're beginning to sound like a spokesperson for the Ministry of Health.'

Megan was still laughing, one hand on her crown, the other wrapped around her second plastic cup of punch—which must be her last drink, at least until something solid went into her stomach—when Robbie whipped out a piece of mistletoe from his pocket and dangled it over her head.

It was so sudden and so unexpected that at first Megan wasn't quite sure what he was doing, waving a leaf above her. But it clicked when his hand went to her waist and he pulled her towards him. With an audience of eighteen people, hooting with laughter, he delivered a kiss worthy of any theatrical performance.

She was tilted backwards at the waist, and it flashed through her mind that it wasn't a very dignified position when wearing the short scarlet dress. One shoe went flying, and as she regained a vertical position, still laughing, with her arm slung around Robbie's neck for balance, she froze at the sight of Alessandro and Victoria standing at the doorway—late arrivals.

What the heck were they doing here?

'We have unexpected company,' she groaned in a mortified undertone.

Robbie followed the direction of her glance and she might have had a little too much to drink, but why did she get the impression that the appearance of Alessandro and his fiancée was not entirely shocking for him?

'Didn't think they would make it,' he murmured, settling

his hand around her waist. He was smiling, leading her towards the door, while the rest of their assembled audience got on with the business of having fun.

Megan wanted the ground to open and swallow her up. This had all the hallmarks of the birthday-cake fiasco, which had been forever branded in her mind as the day romance died. Of course it was a silly notion, because as she now knew, for Alessandro, she had always been an interlude, but it had often seemed easier to pin her misery on that one isolated incident.

And now here she was, in a ridiculous situation all over again, as though she still made a habit of being wild.

She could feel Alessandro's eyes pinned coldly on her face as she paused to stagger into the mislaid red shoe.

And Victoria?

Megan groaned mentally. Great image of the responsible teacher! She was certainly looking a little gimlet-eyed and upset. Probably considering her son's options for changing schools even as she walked towards her.

'You're here!' Megan trilled, plastering a delighted smile on her face. 'Robbie said…' she slapped his hand away from her waist '…you probably wouldn't be able to make it… No nanny…chef having to work in someone else's kitchen… Is Dominic…here…?'

'My mother's joining us for lunch,' Victoria said stiffly, sidestepping Robbie to present Megan with an exquisite box of chocolates. 'I thought it best to leave Dominic at home with her, playing with his toys, and of course, she can supervise Alessandro's chef in the kitchen. We won't stay long.'

'But long enough for a drink, I hope!' Robbie reinserted himself into the picture.

Victoria shook her head and looked at him coolly. 'I don't think so. We really are just popping in, and I wouldn't want to…'

'Don't…' Robbie told her, linking his arm through hers

'…be such a crashing bore. There's some punch lurking somewhere in the kitchen. You're going to have a glass—or should I say a plastic cup…?' He winked at Megan. 'And why don't *you* take care of our other guest, Megan? He looks as though he could do with a bit of loosening up….'

'Quite an outfit.' Alessandro skimmed his eyes lazily over her scantily clad body.

Not only was the dress ludicrously short and ludicrously red, it was also ludicrously revealing. Why was she bothering to wear it at all? he wondered. Unless it was to invite the male eye to follow the generous cleft of her cleavage down to the point where only someone with a stupendous lack of imagination wouldn't be fantasising about what wasn't on show.

'And nice hair.' He reached up and briefly twirled a few red strands between his fingers, so that she jerked back, out of reach. 'Are you supposed to be a scarlet woman?'

'Fancy dress. Of sorts. It's just some cheap hair colour. Tomorrow I shall go back to being blonde. I didn't expect to see you here.'

'I think I'm going to need a drink to handle this…party….'

'Sure. What would you like? There's the usual stuff in the kitchen…' She looked around desperately, to see if she could catch Robbie's eye, but having played perfect host for the past two hours, he had now inconveniently disappeared. 'I'll fetch you something and introduce you round.' She tugged the hem of her dress, as though by doing so she might lengthen it a couple of crucial inches.

'This is just like your university parties, Megan,' Alessandro said, following her towards the kitchen, his hands shoved into the pockets of his casually elegant and totally incongruous dark trousers. 'Cheap booze, loud music…'

'Are you telling me that I haven't grown up?' She spun round and glowered at him.

'If the cap fits…'

'You used to rather enjoy those university parties!' She thrust a cup of punch into his hands and looked at him.

It was a clear, cold morning, and some of the guests had spilled out into the tiny garden, where they had put a rented patio heater in anticipation. Out of the corner of her eye she could see Robbie talking expansively to Victoria, who seemed to have made inroads into the drink she'd claimed she wouldn't be having.

'There's a time and a place for everything.' God, he realised he sounded a bore, but the sight of her literally being swept off her feet by a football coach in a pair of shorts had unsettled him. And he didn't understand why. 'Sure, getting drunk in cheap digs was fine seven years ago—but time moves on.'

'These *digs* are far from cheap, let me tell you, and I am *not* drunk.'

'You could have fooled me. Unless you just enjoy making a spectacle of yourself?'

Megan began doing something with paper plates and cutlery. 'I don't know why you came here, Alessandro. You think I'm immature and silly, and you think Robbie's a loser.' She turned to face him, balancing on both hands as she leant against the kitchen counter. 'Why didn't you go for champagne cocktails and canapés at one of your business colleagues' houses? Where you could have had a civilised drink and talked about the world economy and politics, or the shocking price of houses in London and this year's City bonuses?'

'Because you wouldn't have been there.' Alessandro said it without thinking, and in the tight, ensuing silence he downed his drink, angry with himself for having spoken without thought. In fact, he hadn't even realised that he had been *thinking* that until the words were out of his mouth and it had been too late to take them back.

'You came here…because you *wanted to see me*?' She could feel the slow, treacherous thud of her heart. 'Oh, I'm getting it. You came because you weren't finished preaching to me about how I should live my life. Hence the crack about me being a scarlet woman?'

Relieved to have been let off the hook, Alessandro crumpled the paper cup in one hand and tossed it into a black bin bag which had been thoughtfully hooked over two handles of one of the kitchen doors and was already getting full.

'Well, as a matter of fact, Robbie was only kissing me because he whipped out a piece of mistletoe from his pocket…' She smiled. 'He can't resist being the centre of attention.'

'So I gathered. And he seems to be fine tuning the talent with my fiancée.'

So he *was* still a jealous sort of guy—maybe just better at hiding it now that he was older. The realisation was a let-down.

'Do you mind?'

'Victoria can take care of herself. You…I'm not too sure.'

'*Me?* What does this have to do with *me*, and what gives you the right to gatecrash our party and then start preaching to me about my life choices?' Here, in the small-cluttered kitchen, she could feel his presence crowding her.

'First of all, I did not gatecrash your party.' He needed another drink. There was a bottle of white wine on the counter and he helped himself to another cup. 'Secondly, I recognise that we parted seven years ago on a fairly hostile note—'

'*Fairly hostile?* You tossed me aside like an old shoe that you'd grown sick of. Did you think I was going to smile and be sunshine and light as I conveniently vanished over the horizon? Did you think that I would meet up with you after seven years and welcome you with open arms?' Megan took a deep breath, counted to ten and remembered that this was supposed to be a jolly, relaxing, stress-free day. 'I think we should get back to the party now. There's no point arguing and going over old ground. What happened, happened. We've both moved on with our lives and…'

Alessandro moved towards her, dark, powerful and intimidating without even trying, and Megan watched him jumpily—the way she might have watched a predator circling her, waiting for an opportune moment to pounce.

Which, she berated herself, was a stupid thought, because he happened to be in *her* house, which gave her the right to chuck him out any time she felt like it.

'Have you, though?' he asked in a silky, lazy drawl. 'Really?' He looked at her carefully, aware that this was hardly the right place for a private conversation. At any given moment someone would be sure to barge into the kitchen, on a quest for more drink or food, or just lost because they all seemed to be pretty far gone. 'Because…and here's the thing…I always wondered how you were faring after we broke up….'

'That was very thoughtful of you, Alessandro.' Inside, she was thinking that that was pretty rich, considering she had practically begged to hang on to their relationship at the time.

'Don't you think so?' As he'd expected, she bristled angrily at his glib agreement with her statement. 'Now, having met you again, I worry that you haven't actually moved on as much you keep telling me you have.'

Megan's mouth dropped open at the sheer audacity of that remark, and she did the first thing that came to her head. She picked up a half-full cup of wine that was on the table next to her and flung its contents over his smug face.

He was upon her before she could blink, his hand curled mercilessly around her wrist, his breath warm on her face, sending shivers of apprehension and *horrible, sickening, unwanted, forbidden excitement* racing through her.

'I'm not about to apologise,' she said breathlessly, fixated by his mesmerising eyes.

'Why should you?' Alessandro grated. 'You're angry, and the reason that you're angry is because you know that I speak the truth. You're going out with a guy who's no good for you. He's a flirt, and who knows what he does behind your back?'

'How dare you?'

'I dare because once we were lovers.'

'That's no excuse for you to think you have the right to have an opinion on my life!' Her body, she knew, with anger and frustration, was betraying every sensible protest she was making. Her breasts felt tender, her nipples aching and sensitive in the lacy low-cut bra she was wearing, and there was a heat inside her that was shameful. 'And just because Robbie laughs easily and flirts it doesn't mean that he's running around behind my back, having affairs!' *Why was she still pretending that she and Robbie were an item?* 'He's a great guy....'

'Is he the only man you've had since we broke up?'

'Is Victoria the only woman *you've* had since we broke up?'

She matched his burning gaze with one of her own. This was dangerous territory they were treading. For him it was just a heated exchange, one he felt he had the right to indulge. For her this was a release of passion that threatened to tip over into something else—something for which she would never forgive herself.

'Oh, for goodness' sake! I'm not going out with Robbie,' she confessed unsteadily. 'Okay? I'm not going out with him and never was. We've only ever been good friends.'

'Then why the pretence?' Alessandro released her and stepped back, shaken by what he had felt just then. 'Did you feel that you had to prove something to me?'

Megan was rubbing her wrist, glad of the small distance

he had put between them. At least now her breathing stood a chance of returning to normal.

'Of course I didn't feel that I had to prove anything to you!' She drew in a shaky breath. 'Okay, maybe there was a bit of that. Can you blame me? You suddenly show up and you've got the perfect life—the life you always wanted. You've made your money, and I'm guessing you have a fan club of admirers and people who would bend over backwards to do whatever you want them to do... The past is just some horrible, dusty old memory you've stuck away in a box somewhere... And to top it off you've found the woman of your dreams and you're marrying her... When, by the way? I never asked... When is the wedding set for?'

'We haven't set a date yet.' Alessandro wondered how it was that his perfect life was beginning to feel so damned complicated and *imperfect*. Hadn't he achieved everything he had ever wanted?

'So...' Megan shrugged, and then grinned ruefully— because what was the point getting all worked up when there were people out there having fun?

Perhaps the punch had lowered her defences, making her think that if, now and again, she still had that old familiar pull towards him, then it wasn't that surprising, was it? Everyone carried a certain weakness for their first love.

'Can you blame me if it suited me for you to think that I had a boyfriend? Truth is, I *have* had boyfriends—but not Robbie.' And just in case he took that small confession as a sign that she was somehow still hankering for *him*, she added, 'But as far as not moving on with my life, you couldn't be further from the truth—and it's not just that I've done what I always wanted to do career wise. I learnt a big lesson from you. I really learnt what sort of man I *should* be attracted to... The guys I've gone out with have been kind, funny, smart, caring...'

'Kind, funny, smart, caring… Hmm…Yet the relationships haven't lasted, I take it? Or else one of these wonder men would still be somewhere on the scene…helping little old ladies across roads…making you laugh as he whipped up a soufflé for dinner… having a serious, in-depth conversation about the joys of being broke…'

Megan didn't like where she thought that innocuous remark was heading—and she liked his sarcastic tone of voice even less. 'Sometimes things don't work out. It's no big deal. I mean, I'd rather kiss a thousand frogs on the way to finding my prince.'

'*Kiss a thousand frogs? Find a prince?* What planet are you living on, Megan? That's the sort of cliché an adolescent with starry eyes might come out with! Not that unfailing optimism isn't a heart-warming trait, but haven't you realised by now that life isn't about finding the ideal—it's about learning how to compromise?'

'Is that what you're doing with Victoria, Alessandro? Compromising?'

'I'm using my head, Megan. In life, it's what people do if they are to succeed.'

'Does she know that you're just *compromising*?' Megan found that she preferred the word *compromise* to the phrase *using his head*. *Compromise*, in her eyes, meant that she could remove him from that pedestal of total achievement which he had been so smugly pleased to show her that he occupied. *Compromise* was all about *making do*. No one *compromised* because they wanted to; they *compromised* because they couldn't work out another option.

'Well…' for the first time since she had seen him again after all this time, Megan decided that she could safely occupy the high ground. 'I may be an eternal optimist, but I refuse to *compromise* my emotional life because it *makes sense*. And if I were going out with a man, I'd hate to think that he was only marrying me because it was the *practical* thing to do. As if,' she continued, getting into the swing of things, 'your personal life, the way you feel, can be worked out on a piece of paper like…like a budget!'

Her eyes gleamed with triumph. She was hardly aware that there was a party happening outside—that *her* party was happening outside. She had been vaguely aware of a couple of people entering and leaving the kitchen, but they hadn't interrupted them. An earthquake couldn't have interrupted them.

It was just like when she was young—when sharing the same space as him could hold every fibre of her being captive. She was fixated by the dark, dangerous charisma in his glittering eyes.

It was strange to think that she could just reach out and touch his chest. Accordingly, she had her arms resolutely folded, and her knuckles were white from the pressure of her fingers biting into the soft flesh of her upper arms.

'Well…maybe you're right,' Alessandro drawled softly. 'Maybe the wise thing is to hold out until the search for the perfect mate is successful. Of course, there's always the chance that a person could grow old waiting….'

'It's a risk,' Megan told him airily.

'A risk you're willing to take?'

Megan had a moment of discomfort as she pictured herself getting older and older in the pursuit of Mr Right, until she was a shrivelled up old woman, living on her own, with only a cat for company. She came from a close family unit and had never doubted that she would marry, be happy, have kids— just like her sisters and her parents.

'If it means never settling for second best…'

'And what went wrong with those guys, Megan? The witty, thoughtful ones? Why did *they* fail to measure up? Maybe your standards were a little too high. Do you think that was it?' He smiled slowly. 'Or maybe I set an impossible benchmark….'

'You…*you* are the most *conceited, arrogant*…'

'Yes, yes, yes—but you still haven't answered me….'

Victoria was probably looking at her watch, her eyes darting round in search of him as she tried to avoid the ministrations of the pushy football coach. But Alessandro was hostage to this intense, disquieting conversation. Megan's eyes were blazingly angry, but that didn't faze him. In fact, he wondered how he could have forgotten how passionate and vibrant she was by nature.

'What's there to say? Your benchmark was an upwardly mobile, soon-to-be-a-multi-millionaire guy without a conscience. Fair to say that it's a definite plus if I meet a man who doesn't live up to *that* sterling example.'

'*Upwardly mobile?*'

'What would you prefer, Alessandro? Ambitious to the point of ruthless?'

'Better.'

'You really mean that, don't you?'

'There's nothing wrong with ambition, Megan, and you knew that about me when we were going out. Don't tell me that you saw me sitting in front of books, chasing a Masters degree for the sheer hell of it?'

'No, but at least you were more fun then. Did you get your Masters in the end?'

Alessandro's face was taut with displeasure. It had been a long time since anyone had dared be so outspoken with him. In fact, he thought grimly, he couldn't think of anyone else who had *ever* dared be so outspoken with him—even before he had made his millions and attained his position of invincibility.

'Well?' Megan recklessly flirted with danger, every pore of her being alive to his presence and the heady effect of those glittering dark eyes. 'Are you still in there? Don't tell me that magnificent brain of yours has suddenly decided to hibernate…'

There was a part of her that was very much aware of the quicksand on which she was leaping up and down, but it was a very small part compared to the part that was relishing the feeling of subjecting him to a little criticism on *his* life choices, considering he had been so blasé about criticising *hers*.

He'd hate to be thought a bore. It had always been his most incisive put-down—the one word by which he would casually dismiss someone, out of his sphere. In the past, any lecturer referred to by him as *a bore* had stood the uncomfortable risk of being subjected to Alessandro's verbal wordplay—and Alessandro had never lost even then, even as a young man in his twenties. And now any colleague he considered *a bore* simply became invisible.

'You are getting out of your depth with this conversation, Megan,' Alessandro gritted. His eyes flickered to her, to the cup she was still holding. 'Maybe it's time you called it a day.'

'I've had two cups of punch! I don't think I'll be keeling over any time soon.'

'Two cups too many, judging from your wild antics with the football coach who may not be your lover but might be within your sights. *Is* he?' Alessandro gripped her arm and jerked her towards him.

'Is he what?'

'In waiting for the role of Prince Charming?'

'Of course not! And you're hurting me!'

Alessandro let her go immediately and stepped back, suddenly aware of the build-up of emotion that was flowing between them like a live charge of electricity.

'This isn't what it's about, you know,' he told her, unerringly going for the soft spot in her defences. 'Relationships. Men don't *want* a woman who screams and provokes attack.'

'I get the message,' Megan said, her face burning as she saw herself through his eyes. Punch-drunk, or so he might think. She knew that she wasn't even close to being out of control. Even though he'd seen her being kissed in front of an audience by a man she claimed she had no interest in, aside from a platonic one.

'You might believe in the value of melodrama, but has it occurred to you that for every one man who enjoys that sort of stuff there are a hundred who don't?'

'I wasn't being *melodramatic*. I was just having a bit of fun.' But the fight had gone out of her. She felt like a Cinderella who hadn't quite managed to make it to midnight at the ball.

'I think it's time Victoria and I left now.' Alessandro turned away and headed for the door.

He couldn't believe that he had been totally unaware of the steady thump of music outside, the shouts of laughter emanating from the sitting room and out in the small hallway.

It was a small house, but he still had to hunt down his fiancée, who seemed to be having great fun playing some sort of drinking game with a group of people—including, naturally, the football coach, towards whom Alessandro was beginning to nurture some fairly healthy feelings of hostility.

A regular one-man cabaret show, he thought, grabbing his coat and slinging it on. When he wasn't slobbering over women, he was holding court with a can of beer in one hand and a cup of punch in the other.

He didn't know whether Megan was still in the kitchen or not. He hadn't looked over his shoulder when he had walked out. He would get back to the sanity of Victoria's Chelsea house, enjoy what would be a predictably superb lunch, and then head back to his own place, where he would usefully be able to catch up with some correspondence.

He would not spend the night at Victoria's. He never did. She had made noises about Dominic not being old enough to understand the situation until it was more formalised, and Alessandro was fine with that decision. She occasionally stayed the night at his place, though rarely, and that, too, suited him.

He was congratulating himself on the sanity of his life, on the easy preordained lines along which it ran, when the flicker of red caught his eye.

Even at a distance, and amongst a crowd of colourful people, Megan still managed to stand out. She always had. He shook his head, resigned to polite goodbyes, and walked towards her, his hand resting lightly on the back of Victoria's neck.

'Water!' Megan said, pointedly lifting the paper cup she held. She had had time to gather herself, and wasn't about to let her confrontation with Alessandro wreck her day. People only got under your skin if you allowed them to. She looked at Victoria and laughed. 'I'm afraid your fiancé thinks I'm a disreputable woman, because I've had two cups of punch today.'

This surely wasn't the same uptight, rigid, painfully polite woman she had met at the Nativity Play at school. Her cheeks were flushed and her eyes were sparkling. Maybe *she* had been a little over-indulgent on the punch as well, Megan thought. Poor thing. She'd be in for a stiff lecture on the demon drink.

'I never realised you disapproved of alcohol.' Victoria looked at Alessandro with surprise.

'I don't,' Alessandro said through gritted teeth, 'disapprove of alcohol.'

'Only the effects of it.' Megan smiled sweetly at him and piously sipped some of her water.

'Well…' Victoria laughed—a proper, warm laugh. 'Everyone needs to let their hair down now and again. Now, darling, shall we leave?' She turned to Alessandro, brushing aside his hand in the process and smoothing her hair. 'It was so good of you both to invite us here for a drink. Super party! But my mother will be tearing her hair out if we stay much longer, and I can't imagine what havoc Dominic's been wreaking in my absence! He begged Santa for a football,' she confided.

'And let me guess… Santa obliged…?'

'More than that! Santa managed to get one signed by the captain of the Chelsea team—and of course, Robbie… Mr Chance…' She pinkened. 'His new hero, it would appear….'

'Robbie *can* have that effect on people.' Megan broke with tradition and gave the other woman a quick, warm hug. 'Have a wonderful Christmas lunch…' She sneaked a look at Alessandro, following the movement of his hand as he rested it lightly on Victoria's shoulder, and felt a stab of pure, unattractive, inappropriate *jealousy*. She pulled back as though she had been stung, her face hot. 'Tell Dominic happy Christmas from me. It's been nice…' she smiled stiffly at Alessandro '…catching up. In case I don't see you again, take care!'

And there was no chance then to prolong the farewells, as food was calling. In the sudden confusion of people heading to the kitchen, she was only aware of Alessandro, as he disappeared behind Victoria through the front door and off to his perfect, refined Christmas lunch.

CHAPTER FOUR

For Megan and Charlotte, Christmas lunch was not so much refined as chaotic, noisy and lively. The last guest reluctantly left at a little after seven, and by eight-thirty most of the detritus had been cleared away—or at least channelled into the kitchen to await further action. At which point Charlotte announced that she would be spending the night at her boyfriend's.

Megan was relieved. She was tired, and she wasn't in the mood for a post mortem of the day which would inevitably include lots of questions about Alessandro which Charlotte had been itching to ask ever since he had walked through their front door with Victoria hanging on his arm. She had managed to ask quite a few during the clear-up but Megan knew her friend better than most, and knew that given a few minutes' peace over a cup of coffee in their sitting room, she would move in for the kill.

She had picked up the pieces seven years ago, and had a lot to say on the subject of Alessandro the rat. Hence why Megan had decided to tactfully omit mentioning their initial meeting. The only wonder was that Charlotte had managed to be reasonably polite to him earlier, and that was probably because she had been too busy rushing around.

By nine, then, Megan had the house to herself, and the full weight of her thoughts settled on her shoulders like a burden of lead.

It shouldn't hurt, but seeing Alessandro with Victoria did. It had been one thing to contemplate over the years the sort of life he might have been having, the sort of women he might have been seeing, but to have the reality of his happiness thrust upon her was a bitter pill to swallow.

Worse than that was the fact that he felt sorry for her. And *even worse* than that was the sickening suspicion that she still had feelings for him—that she was still attracted to him even though he had derailed her life once before and ticked none of the boxes in what she considered her mental file of suitable men. He was arrogant, egotistical and driven. She liked shy, genuine and easygoing. But just thinking about him made her feel hot under the collar, and her nervous system seemed to go haywire the minute she was within spitting distance of him.

She wondered what the point of lessons was if you didn't actually learn from them. Alessandro had dispatched her years ago, because he had been moving up and she wasn't suitable to make the journey with him. She had spent a long time hating him, an even longer time trying to rid her system of his memory, and longer still allowing men to re-enter her life— men who were good for her, who boosted her confidence, who never implied, not *once*, that she wasn't good enough.

The two guys she had gone out with had not been earth-shattering affairs, but they *had* been good for her. They had made her realise that there was life beyond the high-octane, high-intensity, high *everything* passion that had consumed her when she had been with Alessandro.

She had managed to reach a vantage point of inner strength. Or so she had imagined. One accidental meeting and here she was, back to emotional free fall.

It seemed ridiculous to still be wearing the small red dress, even though the high-heeled shoes had been dispatched to the black bin liner in the kitchen, along with the green tights. She had a quick shower, changed into track pants, and was doing a last-minute check to find anything that might be lurking behind doors, under sofas or wedged beneath cushions that might reasonably begin to smell unless immediately removed, when she spotted the jacket.

It had probably begun life on the coat hooks by the front door, but the situation with the coats had been a bit of a disaster. Too many of them and not enough hooks. Not enough space altogether by the front door, so some had been removed to one of the bedrooms upstairs, others to the little utility room at the back of the kitchen, and a few hung over the banister. This stray had obviously slipped through and ended up wedged behind the tall earthernware contraption which they used as an umbrella stand.

She shook it out, frowning. A man's jacket, and an expensive one. She could tell immediately from how the fabric felt in her fingers, even with dust covering it. Charcoal-grey, with a deep navy silk lining.

Of course she knew who it belonged to. She knew even before she reached into an outside pocket and extracted one of the business cards with Alessandro's name on it. His name, the name of his company and the various telephone numbers on which he could be reached.

Just looking at his name in elegant black print made her feel shaky.

At a little before ten in the evening there was a high chance that he would be at his fiancée's house. She could, she supposed, always wait until morning, because not even a high-powered, self-motivated, money-making tycoon such as he was needed a jacket at ten in the evening, but she dreaded making the call and would have a sleepless night if she knew that it would be awaiting her in the morning.

She strolled into the sitting room with the business card in her hand, and before she could start convincing herself that she would be better off pretending never to have found the damned jacket, she dialled his mobile number and waited.

The man must have had his phone glued to his ear, because he answered on the second ring, his voice reaching her as though he was standing next to her in the room.

'I have your jacket.' Megan decided straight away that there was no point with pleasantries. 'It's Megan, by the way,' she added.

'I know who it is.' Alessandro pushed back the chair in his office and extended his long legs to rest them on the desk.

He had had an enjoyable Christmas lunch. The food, as expected, had been superb, but the atmosphere had seemed limp after Megan's drinks party. He had met Victoria's mother once before, and she had been as charming as he remembered, but he had found it difficult to concentrate on her conversation, and matters hadn't been helped by Dominic, who had insisted on listing all of the football coach's outstanding qualities, which largely consisted of a willingness to spend limitless time explaining the rules of football to him. He had also offered to take him to a *proper* match, which apparently constituted reasons for immediate sainthood.

The signed football had even accompanied them to lunch, and had been placed reverently on the table next to Dominic, as though expecting to be served turkey with all the trimmings.

Every time Alessandro had looked at it, which had been often because it had been impossible to miss, he'd thought of the man kissing Megan. And every time he'd thought of that, he'd wondered whether she was considering taking him as her lover.

All in all, he had been relieved when, at six, he'd been able to make his excuses and leave.

Victoria had given him a wallet, and he had made all the right noises, but it now lay forgotten in his coat pocket. He would put it in his drawer in the morning, but doubted he would ever use it. He was attached to the one he used, which harked back to his university days. His Megan days.

He hadn't remembered the jacket until now. He had worn his coat over the jacket, and had been in such a hurry to leave that the lack of the jacket hadn't been noticed.

'Where was it?' The computer in front of him was reminding him of the report he had been in the middle of writing, and he swivelled it away from him.

'It must have fallen. I'm afraid it's a bit dirty, because it got stuck behind our umbrella stand.'

'Have your guests all gone?'

'Of course they have, Alessandro. Have you seen the time? Anyway, I won't keep you from your Christmas Day. I just wanted to tell you that I have your jacket, and you can collect it whenever you want.'

'Now might be an appropriate time.'

'Now?' What, Megan wondered, could be so important about a jacket that he would want it right at this very second?

'I don't like putting things off. You know that.' He also knew that he had at least twenty other jackets hanging in his wardrobe, hand-tailored, silk-lined, mega-expensive and totally disposable. 'My driver isn't available at the moment, but I will send a taxi to pick you up. You and my jacket.'

'No, Alessandro. For starters, I don't see why *I* have to be the one to bring you your jacket. It's *your* jacket; *you* can come and fetch it yourself—and anyway, it's too late now. I've spent the past two hours clearing up this house and I'm tired. I want to go to bed.'

She fingered the business card, rolling her thumb over the indented letters of his printed name. She had told herself that she never wanted to lay eyes on him again, that she wouldn't let him ruin her peace of mind, but now, hearing his voice, she was once again reduced to helplessness.

'Fine. I'll be over first thing in the morning to collect it—just in case you have plans for Boxing Day.'

Did she? Victoria would be going to her family in Gloucester for three days, an invitation which he had declined due to his workload. Naturally she had understood perfectly, because she, herself, could hardly spare the time for the short break, but her own absence, she had told him, would be unforgiveable. He had a selection of parties from which he could choose, but he didn't relish any of them. Champagne cocktails, smoked salmon and lots of City talk. Just the kind of thing that Megan had scornfully told him he should have gone to today, instead of imposing his presence on her fun-loving crowd of friends.

No, he would fetch his jacket and then have a quiet day in the company of his computer.

Or rather he would send a taxi to bring Megan and his jacket to him. He found that that was a much more satisfying option.

'No plans to speak of,' Megan was now telling him slowly. 'I shall probably go to the pub with Charlotte and her boyfriend for lunch.' She yawned. 'Anyway…'

Her voice trailed off and he took the hint. He said goodbye and hung up, but even though she had gritted her teeth and spoken to him on the phone, she still wasn't rewarded with a peaceful night's sleep.

She awoke the following morning with a groggy head and an urgent feeling that she had to get ready as quickly as possible, so that she would be ready and waiting at the door with the jacket.

Every time she saw Alessandro she could feel her peace of mind being chipped away—a gradual erosion that frightened her and made her hark back to the days when all he'd had to do was snap his fingers to have her running to him. She would make sure that she was standing at the door when he arrived, with the jacket in one hand and the doorknob in the other, just so that he didn't get any ideas of a pleasant cup of coffee and some more of his killer chit-chat before he headed off. It was a measure of how much he had forgotten her that he could look at her and talk to her and try to set her straight on the facts of life with the polite detachment of a well-meaning but essentially indifferent ex-boyfriend.

Alessandro. Indifference. Was there anything more hurtful than indifference? And was there anything more infuriating than *trying* to be indifferent and failing?

Megan bolted down a very quick breakfast of some left-over quiche washed down with a cup of tea, and was ready, as planned, when the doorbell went at a little after nine.

She strolled to the front door, opened it, and had a polite smile pinned to her face. She was wrong-footed to find a taxi driver grinning back at her.

'Sorry.' Megan dropped the polite smile and frowned. 'I was expecting someone else.'

'I've been asked to collect you and a jacket, I believe, miss?'

'Here's the jacket.'

'My instructions were to bring you as well.'

'Sorry. No can do.'

'Can't return without you, miss. But you can take as long as you like making your mind up 'cos the meter's running. I would really appreciate it if you came, miss, as I'm promised a very generous tip—enough for me to get back home to my family and not be out here on Boxing Day trying to pull fares.'

Megan clicked her tongue in disgust. Alessandro was either

too busy or too lazy to run this boring errand himself, and too suspicious to entrust his measly jacket to a taxi driver, even a black cab driver, a notoriously honest species. No, he would see nothing wrong in dragging her out of her house on Boxing Day, just so that she could chaperon a jacket to his fiancée's house and save him the effort.

'Give me ten minutes,' she said in a seething voice.

She was still seething fifteen minutes later as she sat in the back of the cab with the precious jacket on her lap, bitterly regretting her decision to phone him when she should have just stuffed it back in its cubbyhole and waited for Charlotte to make the discovery. Which she would have. In due course. Possibly after a month or two.

London was a different place when the roads were clear and the pavements relatively free of pedestrians. In an hour or so when some of the big stores opened, people would once more venture out of their houses in search of early sales bargains, but at the moment it was possible to appreciate the graceful symmetry of the buildings as the taxi took her away from Shepherd's Bush and towards Chelsea.

She had no idea where Victoria and Dominic lived, but she wasn't surprised when the cab pulled up outside a tall, redbrick house with neat black railings outside. The value of the property could be guessed by the quality of the cars parked on the street outside, and the peaceful, oasis-like feel of the area. This might not be a rural idyll, but it was London life at its most elegant.

She followed the cab driver up to the regal black front door with its gleaming brass knocker and banged it twice. It was opened almost immediately—and not by Victoria.

'Ah. You've brought my jacket.'

Megan looked at Alessandro and scowled.

'You could have come and fetched it yourself,' she told him, holding up the precious cargo.

He didn't answer as he paid the taxi driver, and from the exchange of notes, Megan wasn't at all surprised that the cab driver had been anxious for her to accompany him with the jacket. The tip looked sufficient to fund a two-week family holiday somewhere hot.

'Here you are.' She stuck her hand out. In return, Alessandro stood aside and motioned her in. Megan stayed put. 'Thanks, but I have to go.'

'How did I know that you would say that?' He began walking inside, and knew she had followed him by the slam of the front door. 'You've become very predictable,' he threw over his shoulder.

'Where's Victoria?' Megan demanded, stopping short by the door and looking past his retreating back for other signs of life.

The hallway was airy and gracious, with gleaming wooden flooring complementing the gleaming wooden banisters that led up the stairs. It was an old house that had obviously been renovated to the highest possible modern standard. Suspiciously, there was no sign of a Christmas tree anywhere. Nor were there any signs of toys, which she would have expected to have seen lying around in the wake of a small, over-indulged boy on Boxing Day.

'At her own house, I would imagine.' Alessandro turned to look at where she was still hovering by the front door, clutching the jacket which, six months ago, had been so reverently handled by his tailor in the City.

'Where am I?'

'At my house, of course. Where else did you imagine I would be?'

'What are you doing here?'

'I live here.'

'I *thought* I would be delivering this to Victoria's house!'

'Did you? Maybe I should explain.' He walked towards her,

reached out and relieved her of the jacket. 'I don't do nights at Victoria's house. She's of the opinion that Dominic wouldn't understand the concept of a live-in lover.'

'Why have you brought me here?'

It was a very good question, and one which Alessandro struggled to answer. Why would he choose to jeopardise his orderly life by courting conversation with a woman who had made it clear that she didn't want to converse with him? Their recent meetings had been tense and unproductive, but it was as though something bigger than him was driving him on to see her.

He didn't know whether it was because the guilt he had felt seven years ago when they had broken up had never really left him—was, in fact, resurfacing, forcing him to try and put things right between them—or whether, having once possessed her so fully that she would have jumped through hoops for him, he couldn't deal with the fact that she now hated his guts. Maybe he needed to convince her that he wasn't the bad guy she thought he was. Although he couldn't work out why it should matter. When had he ever cared about anybody else's opinions? Even an ex-girlfriend's?

Victoria had no problems with him seeing Megan. In fact, she had been positively encouraging on the subject. But how long before she picked up on the strange electricity that still seemed to connect them? How long before that became a problem?

'I don't want you to have a problem with me,' Alessandro told her bluntly. 'Yes, I know you think I'm a bastard who dumped you, but, face it, there'll be times when we bump into one another. You teach Dominic; I am involved with his mother. Therefore I will see you occasionally at school. Presumably.'

He frowned, and wondered why he was having trouble imagining any routine of domesticity with Victoria and her son. He had had no such problem when he had mooted his marriage proposal to her three months previously. At that time he had been comfortable with the notion of settling down with an un-demanding, highly motivated wife who would complement his lifestyle, and allow it to carry on with seamless ease.

'It is ridiculous that we clash every time we meet—and please don't tell me that it is unavoidable. You're choosing to make things difficult between us, and I want us to iron out the creases.'

Megan had figured out why he wanted to 'iron out the creases'. A smooth relationship between them would mean, for him, an easy conscience—and he was right. They prob-ably *would* bump into one another from time to time as he became absorbed into the routine of family life with Dominic and his mother. The school was very hot on parental involve-ment, and sooner or later their paths would cross. An atmo-sphere between them could create all kinds of gossip.

She could jack in her job and look for another one, but that thought lasted all of one second. There was no way she was going to alter her life because she couldn't handle seeing him.

'And that's why you dragged me over here? So that you could try and *iron out creases*?'

'Stop fighting me!'

'Is that an order? Have you become so accustomed to obe-dience, Alessandro, that you can't stand the thought of anyone refusing to bow, and scrape, and do exactly as you say?'

'You never obeyed me, Megan.' He gave her a crooked smile, remembering the way she had been able to tease him out of studying, had laughed when he had frowned at some of her micro-mini skirts, and coaxed him into going to gigs with her even though he had hated most of the bands.

Megan wanted to ask him whether that was why he had seen no future in their relationship—because he hadn't imag-ined her in the role of obedient wife. But then she thought that there had probably been a hundred reasons why he had seen no future in their relationship, and asking for a breakdown of them would just be taking yet another stupid step into a past that was best left behind.

In the end he was right when he said that she was fighting him. What he didn't realise was that she was also fighting herself, for still having misplaced feelings towards him.

Right now, for instance, even though he had dragged her from the comfort of her own house at his bidding, she still felt achingly *aware* of the stark dynamism of his personality, the sexy, lean magnetism of his hard-boned face and muscular body. He was wearing a pair of black running pants and a black tee shirt. It had always been his uniform for relaxation, and he looked as much at ease wearing them now, in the expensive splendour of his Chelsea home, as he had in the squalor of his one-bedroom rented studio flat.

She wondered how long it would take him to realise that her prickly reaction to him was as much to do with her as it was to do with him. He had almost hit the bullseye when he had told her, mockingly, that maybe the memory of him had prevented her from finding a replacement, but he hadn't pursued that line of thought.

She shuddered to think how he would react if he ever realised how close he'd been to the truth.

'You're right.' She gave him a wry smile—an olive-branch smile. 'I think the word you used to use was *stubborn*.'

'Like a mule,' Alessandro agreed.

'Not one of life's most attractive animals.'

Alessandro couldn't recall having had a problem with finding her as sexy as hell, whatever stubborn traits she had had. In fact, he *still* found her as sexy as hell. In a purely objective way, he told himself. The red had been washed out of her hair, which was now back to pure pale blonde, and was doing what it had always done: refusing to buckle under the control of clips and a hair tie.

'Stay for coffee?'

'Maybe a quick one. You have a fabulous house, Alessandro. How…um…how long have you lived here?'

He couldn't resist teasing her. 'Um…four years….'

'I was just being polite!' She told herself not to bristle, but when he looked around at her, he was grinning. When he chose to bring it out, he had a smile that could knock anyone sideways. He was bringing it out now. 'How was your Christmas Day?' she asked, retreating to the least offensive topic she could think of.

'Well…' Alessandro's kitchen was a marvel of black granite and chrome. He reached into a cupboard for a couple of mugs and began making them a pot of coffee. 'I went to a very good drinks party in the morning….'

'Oh, really? And what would you describe as *very good*?' There were three stools tucked under one of the kitchen counters and Megan perched on one, swivelling it around so that she could look at him as he poured boiling water into mugs. Even the kettle looked like something out of a spaceship. Very high-tech. 'Do you mean that there was caviar and champagne? Smoked salmon on brown bread? Stuff like that?'

'I can tell you don't move in wealthy circles, Megan.' He handed her a mug and pulled out the stool next to hers. 'And before you jump down my throat, all I'm saying is that smoked salmon and caviar are a bit old hat now.'

'I'm disappointed. I've always wanted to chance my luck with a bit of caviar. Guess I missed the boat. So, what was this fabulous drinks party like, then?'

'Very…energetic. The hostess, unfortunately, didn't appreciate my presence.' He took a sip of coffee and looked at her over the rim of his mug. 'Or if she did, she wasn't showing it.'

God, he was beautiful. Long, thick eyelashes…sexy eyes…the curve of his mouth…

She snapped out of it and remembered that this was what being friendly was all about. It was conversing without edginess, and without dredging up past hurts and recriminations.

She also reminded herself that he was engaged to be married.

'She was probably just a little startled to see you there. Did you have a delicious Christmas lunch?' she asked.

Alessandro shrugged. 'One superb meal tastes much like another.' Just like making the last million was much like making another. Only the first ever really counted. He looked at the heart-shaped face, the big, blue, almond-shaped eyes looking back at him, the full, kissable mouth.

'Oh, to be able to say that!' She felt a slight shift in the atmosphere and awkwardly edged her way off the stool. 'I really should be going now.'

Caught up in the meanderings of his own thoughts, Alessandro frowned.

He didn't want her to go.

What the hell did *that* mean?

Cutting through all the reasons he had given himself for his inexplicable urge to keep seeing her in the face of her obvious reluctance to see *him*—the guilt factor…the altruistic concern for her welfare…the practicality of having a civilised relationship because they would meet up occasionally as a matter of course—cutting through all that, like a dark undercurrent under the placid surface of a lake, lay the disturbing realisation that he still found her attractive, still found his eyes drifting along her body, remembering the exquisite sexual pleasure she had once afforded him.

Where did that leave Victoria?

He would have to talk to her. He owed it to both of them. But it was just as well that Megan was going.

When, as she approached the front door, she turned around and said politely that, at the risk of repeating herself, she probably *wouldn't* be seeing him any time soon, and to take care and *have a good life*—whatever the hell that meant—he inclined his head in agreement.

That brief window of easy companionship was fading fast. She could see it in his eyes. She wasn't sure what she had interrupted—work, probably—but he was eager to have her gone now, so that he could get back to whatever he had been doing.

She had wondered whether she had never been obedient enough. Now she suspected that she had just been tiresome. Suddenly she wanted to get away as fast as her legs could take her.

She gabbled something about his jacket needing dry cleaning.

'No need. I will call a taxi for you.'

'No! Thank you. Public transport…'

'Don't be ridiculous! The bus and tube service today will be extremely limited.'

He picked up the jacket and there it was—that tiny weight nestling in the concealed pocket on the inside. He could feel it because it was where he often kept his own cellphone, and it was where he had stashed Victoria's yesterday. He had completely forgotten about it—even when, over Christmas lunch, she had asked him, frowning, whether he knew where she had left it.

It just went to prove how much seeing Megan again had made him take his eye off the ball.

'I have a phone here….'

He flipped the lid and stared at five messages, opened them, read them, and continued staring at the innocent little metal object in the palm of his hand.

'What's up?'

Reminded of her presence, Alessandro looked at her distractedly

'The taxi…?' Megan prodded nervously, because he was now staring at her in a really odd way and she figured that the egg timer that measured his patience levels was beginning to run perilously low. She would imprint this memory in her brain for ever, she told herself fiercely. It would do her well to remember, should she ever start going down the nostalgia road again, that she could outstay her welcome in a very short space of time.

She backed towards the door, but she doubted he even really noticed. He looked as though he were a million miles away.

'Yes. The taxi.' Alessandro snapped shut the phone and shoved it in the pocket of his sweats. 'Might be quicker if I walk out with you and hail one.'

'Are you sure you're okay, Alessandro?'

'What? Yes,' he told her irritably. 'Why? Are you planning on getting your Florence Nightingale hat on if I'm not?'

'There's no need to jump down my throat,' Megan snapped back, pulling on her coat. 'I only asked.'

'Because underneath that thin veneer of hating my guts you still really care about my well-being, right?' He clenched his fist round Victoria's cellphone, burning a hole in his pocket, and willed his legendary self-control back into place. 'I'm being rude. Apologies. You did me a favour bringing my jacket, and for that I thank you.'

'No problem,' Megan said coolly. They were out in the street now and there was no sign of him feeling the cold, even though the wind was brisk and the skies promised freezing rain later.

She had to half run to keep pace with him as he headed towards the Kings Road—which, predictably, was already crowded with restless shoppers, who were clearly bored with enforced inactivity.

Tellingly, he wasn't even glancing in her direction. She might almost have not existed at all. So much for the friendly truce. Once established, he obviously saw no need to prolong it.

He managed to hail a taxi with the efficiency of a magician pulling a rabbit out of a hat, and Megan couldn't dash towards it fast enough.

'How much?' Alessandro reached for his wallet and Megan looked at him with freezing disdain.

'I can pay for this myself,' she told him flatly. 'Teachers may not be the highest-paid workers in the city of London, but we can still run to the occasional taxi fare.'

'Be quiet, Megan, and get in the cab. This is a journey you undertook for my benefit, so don't waste your time arguing about something as pitiful as the cost of a cab ride to Shepherd's Bush.'

He was already fishing out the amount quoted, and handed it over while Megan glared at him, confused and stung by his abrupt change of mood.

She sat back and stared straight ahead in total silence, half expecting him to say something. *Anything.*

He didn't. He pushed himself away from the taxi, and as she turned her head she saw him quickly disappearing as he half-jogged back to his house.

It had been a learning curve, she told herself brightly as the cab driver pulled away. Learning curves were very important, and this particular learning curve had come at a very opportune moment. Because he had catapulted back into her life and shattered her peace of mind. But now, she told herself, staring out of the window at the grey, uninspiring view rolling past her, she could consider herself on the road to recovery.

Firstly, she had seen Alessandro and Victoria together in a social situation, and instead of letting her mind drift away into the past she would now have it cemented in her head that Alessandro was half of a couple. She might call it a compromise relationship, but it was still very real and very meaningful for him.

Secondly, she had seen for herself how impatient he could become with her—because really and truly he *had* outgrown her.

Thirdly, she had proved conclusively to herself that she could actually have a normal conversation with him—which surely meant that he was no longer the bogeyman in her head, the guy who had broken her heart, the benchmark against whom all other men fell short.

Fourthly... She couldn't think of a fourthly, but she would.

She thought of him back in his house, looking through her and past her as if she had suddenly become invisible.

The best Christmas present she could give herself would be a gift-wrapped box full of all those reminders of why it was time to finally let Alessandro go.

CHAPTER FIVE

ALESSANDRO stepped out of his car, dispatched his driver, and squinted through the driving rain at Megan's house. There were several reasons why he shouldn't be here—the most pressing one being that he had had too much to drink. It was also gone eleven in the night. A time when most normal people would be tucked up in bed. But he'd banked on Megan not being in the *normal* category, and sure enough there were lights on.

He didn't give himself too much time to think. Lately, thinking hadn't been doing him too much good.

He began walking very slowly up to the front door. He could feel the icy rain slashing against his face, permeating through the thin layers of his trenchcoat and jumper to bare skin.

The three bangs he gave on the front door were loud enough to raise the dead. There was a muffled sound of activity, and the door was pulled open just as he had raised his hand to administer another earth-shaking bang.

'Oh, my God. What are *you* doing here?'

'Developing pneumonia.' Alessandro placed the palm of his hand on the door—at which point Charlotte positioned herself neatly between him and the hallway. 'Let me in.'

'Megan's not here.'

Alessandro pushed a little harder and stepped forward. 'You're as forthright as ever, aren't you?'

'Just looking out for my friend, and she doesn't want to see you.'

'Doesn't want to see me or isn't in? Make your mind up.'

The appearance of Megan hovering on the staircase behind Charlotte answered at least one of his questions. She looked confused and rumpled, as though she had just woken up. Her cheeks were flushed, and her silky blonde hair was a curly cloud around her startled face.

'Alessandro! What on earth are *you* doing here?'

'Have both of you learnt your lines from the same script? I'm getting soaked.'

'Do you know what time it is?'

Alessandro made a cynical pretence of consulting his watch. His head was beginning to throb.

'Just open the damned door, Megan! Please.'

It was the *please* that did it. Alessandro had never made a habit of doing *please*, and to hear it dragged out of him now warned her that something was very wrong. She elbowed Charlotte aside, like a master nudging back a very loyal dog determined to keep all visitors at bay.

'Shall I stay, Megan?' Charlotte's arms were folded, and she was looking at Alessandro's dripping figure with narrow-eyed suspicion.

'No, no. It's okay. I'll just hear what he wants and he'll be on his way.'

'Well, if you're *sure*…' Her voice implied that one false move would have her bounding down the stairs pronto, but she grudgingly left—though not before giving Alessandro an evil look out of the corner of her eye.

Her departure didn't mean that he was warmly welcomed in. In fact, Megan had now adopted her friend's pose, arms folded, her big blue eyes narrowed, her mouth drawn into a tight, suspicious line.

'I need to get out of these clothes.'

'You need to tell me what you're doing here.'

'I thought we'd agreed to a ceasefire, Megan.'

'We have. But that doesn't mean that you can stroll in here at close to midnight. We might have called a ceasefire, Alessandro, but we haven't suddenly become best friends.' She was remembering the way he had looked straight through her two days before—as if she had ceased to exist.

Alessandro didn't answer. Instead he began removing his drenched trenchcoat, which he slung over the banister. Megan immediately removed it, holding it up between her fingers as if wary that it might be contaminated.

'The coat hooks are behind you.'

'I need to get out of these things.'

'Why are you so wet?'

'Have you had a look through your window? It's pouring. And,' he added grudgingly, 'I went for a walk before coming here to see you. If I stay in these clothes, I'm probably going to end up in hospital. Would your conscience be able to deal with that?'

He had played successfully on her greatest weak spot, and Megan hesitated. 'All right. If you wait in the sitting room, I'll go and fetch you... Look, just wait, and I'll be down in a minute.'

'Is there a fire in there?'

'No, Alessandro. No roaring open fire. But you can stand very close to the radiator and hope for the best.'

Her nerves were jangling as she took the stairs two at a time, briefly popping in to satisfy Charlotte's avid curiosity. She wasn't sure what she was supposed to provide by way of clothing for him, but after a few hesitant seconds she pulled out a box from under her bed and removed a pair of his sweats, seven years old, and a rugby shirt, also seven years old. Relics of a time past which she had hung on to.

With both items of clothing in her hand, and a clean towel fetched from the airing cupboard, she flew back down the stairs to find him in the sitting room—where he had stripped down to his boxers.

'Wh-what are you doing…?' she stammered, screeching to a halt in the doorway. It was seven years since she had last seen him like this, and his physique had barely changed at all. She stared, mesmerised, looked away, and then covertly looked back at his magnificent body. Wide shoulders tapered to lean hips and long, muscular legs. He was bronzed from head to toe, and without benefit of clothes every sinewy muscle was evident.

'Taking off my wet clothes.'

Megan cleared her throat and dragged her eyes away from his body to the relative safety of his face. Then she tossed the clothes and towel in his general direction.

'I don't bite, Megan.' Alessandro stooped to pick up the sweats and rugby jumper, which he held up and stared at with open curiosity. 'Bloody hell.'

Megan reddened and stood her ground.

'Are these *mine*?' Alessandro looked past them to her, and for the first time in nearly two days he felt good—really good. Stupidly good.

'They were at my apartment when we broke up. I couldn't face bringing them back to you, and I figured you wouldn't miss them anyway.' She laughed shortly, remembering how she had pressed her face against the fabric, hoping to hold the scent of him. 'I guess I hung on to them for sentimental reasons.'

'What else did you keep?'

'That's all there is, Alessandro. You'd better get dressed.' She turned away and leaned against the doorframe, her profile sideways to him. 'I don't feel comfortable about this…having you here in my house…getting changed…it's not right. I know you've said that Victoria isn't possessive, but I like her and it's not fair on her…'

Alessandro didn't say anything for a while, then, 'It's safe to look now. I'm fully dressed.'

'So why have you come here?' Megan could feel the pulse in her throat beating, mirroring the steady, nervous thump of her heart. She'd been reading in bed, almost ready to switch off the bedside light, when the thumping on the front door had had her flying into her dressing gown. Now she felt wide-awake.

Alessandro strolled over to the sofa and sat down heavily.

'Have you been drinking, by any chance?'

'Stop hovering by the door. I told you. I don't bite. I've come here because I need to talk to you, and I can't talk to you when you're standing there like a sergeant major on duty.'

'I should put your wet clothes in the drier. It'll only take twenty minutes for them to dry.'

She tentatively took a few steps towards the pile of soggy clothes, snatched them up, and then fled to the utility room, where she stuck them in the drier. Twenty minutes on the highest setting. For a few seconds she leaned against the tumble drier, eyes closed, then she took a few deep breaths and headed back to the sitting room.

This time she saw him sprawled on the sofa. He looked bone weary. Megan walked across and stood over him, until he opened his eyes and looked back at her.

'Victoria and I are finished,' he said.

'You're *what*?'

'And, to answer your previous question a few minutes ago, yes, I've been drinking—but I'm not drunk. Two whiskies—admittedly in rapid succession.'

'So you've come here to carry on drowning your sorrows?' Megan said with heavy sarcasm.

'Don't you want to know *why* Victoria and I have broken up?'

'I don't want to get wrapped up in your personal life, Alessandro.' *She did.* Her voice was saying all the right things, but her head was singing a different song. It was telling her that she wanted to sit down and hear every grisly detail of why he had broken up with the perfect woman.

'Well, you don't have much choice. Because you need to know.'

'What are you talking about?'

'Sit down.'

Megan looked around her and pulled up the closest chair to the sofa. It was an ancient nursing chair, with a low seat and a buttoned back, covered in the worst possible shade of mustard-yellow. It had been donated to her by an aunt. Unsightly, but very comfortable.

'That's better.' Alessandro looked at her and wondered where to begin and how much he should say. 'Did you miss me?' he asked, staring at her and watching the colour climb into her cheeks—watching, too, her pointless efforts to appear in control. 'After we'd broken up? Did you miss me?'

'What's the point of these questions?'

'Just answer.'

'What do *you* think? Yes. I missed you. Is that what you wanted to hear?'

Alessandro gave her one of those smiles that had always been able to make her toes curl.

'It'll do. Did you ever imagine that we'd meet again?'

'No, of course I didn't.' The shadows cast by the side light played lovingly on the hard angles of his face, softening them. His eyes were lazy and watchful. Lying there in his old university clothes, Megan could almost believe that time had moved backwards.

'Nor did I,' Alessandro admitted roughly. 'Not that I didn't wonder what you were up to. I never imagined that you would have come down to England, and definitely not to London.'

'I know. Because I was a country bumpkin meant to stay in the country.'

'Because you always made such a big deal about the horrors of city living. If you'd wanted a change, you could have chosen anywhere else—any green and pleasant pasture somewhere on the outskirts of a city. I never imagined you'd dive right in at the deep end.'

'Blah, blah, blah, Alessandro. I've heard it all before. If you came here to offload, then go ahead. Tell me what happened between you and Victoria, and then you'll have to go. How did you get here anyway? You didn't drive, did you?'

'My driver's gone.'

'So you mean you came here and got rid of your driver, so that now you're at the mercy of finding a cab? At this time in the night?'

'We're getting off topic.'

He reached out and took hold of her hand, curling his long fingers around hers. It was a simple, spontaneous gesture that made her freeze. His fingers were softly stroking hers and his eyes were on her face, staring at her with unblinking intensity.

'What are you doing?' Megan whispered. This indistinct question should have been accompanied by her whipping her hand out of reach, setting out once and for all her basic ground rules, which were that she wanted nothing to do with him. Instead, her hand refused to budge.

'What does it look like? I'm touching you. Do you like it?'

Megan cleared her throat. 'I don't think…' she began, but her voice trailed off as he began stroking the soft underside of her wrist with one finger. It sent shivers racing up and down her body and threw her already confused mind into even more of a state of flat-out panic.

'That's good.'

'What is…?'

'Not thinking.' He lowered his magnificent eyes and watched his finger as it traced tiny circles on her wrist. She was wearing an old pink dressing gown, and he would swear that it was the same one that she'd used to wear at university. Same colour anyway. She had always liked pink. 'Just going with the flow. I thought a lot. I thought that Victoria was the perfect woman for me. I thought she complemented me in every way possible. And, more importantly, I thought she was eminently suitable because she didn't stress me out.'

'So I believe you've told me before.'

'What are you wearing under your dressing gown?'

Megan told herself that she didn't want to hear these questions, she didn't want him looking at her like that, and she definitely didn't want his fingers like a branding iron on her skin. But she wasn't pulling away, was she? And this wasn't just about being kind to a fellow human being who was upset. For starters, she couldn't imagine Alessandro ever *being* upset, at least not upset in the way most normal people would be. Nor was he just another *fellow human being*.

'Will you let me see?' he continued.

'See what?'

He didn't answer that one. Instead he raised his hand to push aside the opening of her dressing gown, and Megan gasped as the flat of his hand came into direct contact with her breast and brushed against the nipple, which stiffened and throbbed *and wanted more*.

'Alessandro, *no!*' She pulled back and shot to her feet, but she was shaking all over. 'I'm sorry your relationship with Victoria hasn't worked out,' she said shakily, clutching her gown together as though it might open up of its own accord unless forcibly restrained. 'And now that you're here I guess

I'm willing to hear your sob story. But don't think that you can come here and expect me to be your consolation prize.'

'Come back and sit down,' was all he said.

'I'm not coming anywhere near you!'

'I'll keep my hands to myself.'

Megan looked at him dubiously. He now had his hands behind his head and, God, she couldn't believe how much she still wanted him. He lay there as beautiful as some classical statue, brought to life by a vengeful God who wanted to mess with her head by dangling temptation in front of her.

'You'd better,' she warned him unsteadily. 'Or else I'll scream and Charlotte will come rushing down the stairs....'

'Like a rottweiler on the loose, ready to chew me to bits…? Since when did *you* ever need a keeper? Okay, okay. I'll tell you my sob story and we can take it from there.'

Take what from where? Megan tried to fathom out what exactly he meant by that, but her brain wasn't functioning properly. She gingerly went back to the chair, but pushed it away a couple of surreptitious inches.

'Victoria,' he told her heavily, 'seemed the perfect solution. Intellectually challenging and on the same wavelength as me. I never thought that *you* would come along and throw everything out of joint. I made it my aim to have a life that yielded to my absolute control. I hadn't bargained on the element of surprise.'

Megan fought hard to remain indifferent, but that was sweet, sweet music to her ears.

'Throw everything out of joint?' she encouraged. 'Element of surprise? What do you mean?'

Alessandro raised his eyebrows. The look in his eyes told her that he knew exactly where she was going with her apparently concerned question. 'Fishing?' he drawled, and Megan flushed. 'No matter. You want me to explain—I'll explain. You made me question whether I had overestimated the notion of *suitability.* I'd forgotten how...*stimulating*...you could be. I'd also forgotten how good we were together...sexually.'

The music was getting sweeter all the time.

'Do you like hearing that?'

'I don't care much one way or the other,' Megan lied airily.

'Don't lie. You forget how well I know you. I saw you, and it didn't take me long to realise that there was still something between us. I know you felt it too.'

'You're imagining things.'

'Am I? Why don't you come and sit a little closer to me, and then you can say that again.' He sat up so that they were facing one another, and she could hear her treacherous heart beating like a drum inside her. 'I decided that it was no good pretending that I wasn't attracted to you, and it was no good being engaged to one woman when I was very busy thinking about another one.'

'You were thinking about *me*?'

'Thinking about you,' he confirmed. 'And thinking about what I wanted to do to you.' He smiled another one of those smiles. 'The minute I saw you at that school play you got inside my head and I couldn't get you out. Every time I looked at you, I imagined taking your clothes off and touching you. Everywhere.'

'I don't believe you.'

'Yes, you do—and if you don't, ask yourself this. Why is it that we've managed to meet up so many times since then? I didn't have to come to that football game you were playing. I didn't have to come to your drinks party on Christmas Day.'

'Stop it!'

The silence stretched between them, dangerous and alive.

'You came to that football game with Dominic and Victoria,' Megan told him shakily. 'And you came to the Christmas Day party with Victoria.'

'But I *came*. There was no need for me to. I could just as easily have stayed away from both, but I didn't. The pull to see you was too strong.'

'If I hadn't shown up, Alessandro, you would still be happily engaged to Victoria. You would be making plans for your wedding…' Megan fought to hang on to a bit of sanity.

'Are you telling me that you didn't feel the same pull towards me? That you haven't once thought of me since fate threw us back together?'

'That's not the point.'

Alessandro swung his long body off the sofa and began prowling through the room. Megan twisted round to follow him with her eyes. Every nerve in her body was on fire. Faced with a reality she had never envisaged, she literally didn't know how to respond. She knew, though, that coming here would not have been something he would have undertaken lightly. Alessandro had had his whole life mapped out from the age of twenty-four. He had chosen Victoria because he would have seen her as slotting in with his long-term plans. To have his own predetermined destiny hijacked would have taken a lot, and for that she was prepared to give him credit.

But giving him credit still didn't tell her what she should do. So she remained silent…watching him as he stopped in front of the bookshelves, idly reached down for a book and leafed through it before slotting it back into its space…looking as he paused to inspect the pictures in their frames, of her and Charlotte, of her and her family, of Charlotte and her family…

Her thoughts were all over the place.

Finally he stopped right in front of her and then leaned forwards, his hands resting on either side of the chair and trapping her so that she had to push herself away.

'Tell me that's not the point, Megan, and I'll walk out of that door and you'll never see me again.'

Up until that moment she had managed, more or less, to persuade herself that she was much better off without Alessandro in her life—that the cruel trick fate had played on her could be remedied by just walking away from him or at least taking strenuous efforts to ensure that she didn't bump into him. Then she had told herself that she could do even better than that…she could rise above the situation and be on civil speaking terms with him *just in case* they *did* bump into one another in the course of events. It had all made perfect sense.

Now, though, as she faced his ultimatum, the reality that he would once again disappear was like looking into a deep, black, bottomless hole. He was deadly serious as he looked straight into her eyes. All she had to do was tell him to go and he would. For good.

Furthermore, it would be *her* choice. It had been bad enough when he had finished their relationship the first time, but at least then she had been the wronged party, and even with herself had come out tops with the sympathy vote. In the space of a few heartstopping seconds she had a glimpse of a future filled with never-ending unanswered *what if* questions.

'I came here because you need to know that I still want you, but I'll walk away, Megan, unless you tell me that you feel the same way about me.'

'I… I… Um…' *I don't want to be hurt all over again!*

'Fine,' Alessandro gritted. 'I get the message loud and clear. Whether you're attracted to me or not doesn't matter. You're still wrapped up in the past and you can't forget it.' He pushed himself up while Megan remained frozen in her chair, looking at him as he began dialling into his mobile phone. He would be calling a taxi. Or getting his long-suffering chauffeur back to collect him. Either way, it amounted to him leaving.

'I'll keep these clothes,' he said with a cynical twist to his mouth. 'You can keep the suit. Or you can just chuck it.'

He turned away from her, heading for the door. Seeing him leave galvanised her into action.

'Don't go!'

At that, Alessandro turned slowly around to face her.

'I…I want you to stay,' Megan said.

The words had a familiar ring about them, but she shoved that to the back of her mind. She had been nineteen when she had last begged him to stay! She was twenty-six now, and anyway she wasn't, she told herself, *begging* him to stay. At least not the way she once had when he had been her entire universe and she had wanted to follow him to the ends of the earth.

'But on my terms,' she added, as he began walking towards her.

'Which are…?'

'That…that…it's just about the sex. Okay, I admit I'm still attracted to you, but I don't want to get *involved* with you…' What a joke. She had never *not* been involved with him, but she had learnt a thing or two about self-defence, and the first rule, she thought now, was to keep that vulnerable side to herself. But somehow, some way, she had to get over this incredible pull of attraction between them. An attraction that was driving her crazy.

'Sex without involvement… After my mistakes with Victoria, I'm all in favour of those terms…' He cupped her face with his hands and stroked her cheeks with his thumbs. Her skin was soft, like satin, and touching her was hauntingly and erotically familiar. 'Shall we go up to your bedroom, or is your keeper going to hear us and come out swinging a heavy object?'

'She's not *that* protective!' Megan felt as though she was on the edge of a precipice, with one foot dangling over the side.

'We could always stay down here,' Alessandro murmured. 'Although the sofa might prove challenging for me, and somehow making love after seven years in front of a radiator instead of an open fire just doesn't seem…' for a minute he almost said *romantic enough* '…to fit the bill…'

They went to her bedroom like a couple of teenagers stealthily trying not to wake the adults—although Charlotte wasn't in the room next door. In fact, the bathroom and airing cupboard separated their rooms, and the house, while small, was old, and hence the walls were thick. Unless they made a great deal of noise, there was no chance that she would wake up.

The minute the bedroom door was shut they faced one another, each absorbing the reality of the decision they had made.

'Shall I tell you what I want to do?' Alessandro murmured huskily. 'I want to rip your clothes off and take you right here, right now, against the wall… But God, Megan, I won't— because I want to enjoy every inch of your glorious body slowly…' He stood back, breathing heavily. He had never been so turned on in his life before, and he didn't dare touch her—not yet, not until his body was ready to behave itself.

He removed the rugby shirt. They had switched on the overhead light, but now Megan went across to her chest of drawers and lit the three scented candles which had permanent residence in her bedroom.

'I see you still have that bad habit,' Alessandro admonished, but with a smile in his voice.

She was smiling too when she replied, 'I know, I know. Fire hazard. But don't they smell wonderful?' She looked at him across the width of the small bedroom. It had seemed all wrong before to look at him, to look at him, but now there were no such limits, and she feasted her eyes greedily on his powerful body, like a starving person suddenly offered the vision of a banquet. When it came to male perfection he had broken the mould. His arms were strong and sinewy, his broad shoulders tapering to a narrow waist which led down to…to…

Megan drew in her breath, shuddering, as he began removing the sweatpants and then his boxer shorts.

'Are we taking turns?' Alessandro asked, oozing satisfaction as he watched her helpless reaction to his nudity. His very *turned-on* nudity. Having her look at him was almost as much of a turn-on as having her touch him, and both ranked second place to *him* touching her.

He strolled towards her double bed and lay down with one hand behind his head enjoying watching her watching him.

'Okay. Start with the robe. But do it very, very slowly…'

God, this felt so damned good, lying here on her bed, looking at her as she peeled off the pink dressing gown to reveal the pyjamas she still wore. He had never been able to persuade her to abandon the habit, and he was beginning to think that there might well be something in it—because he was certainly getting a massive buzz, watching her as she took off first the striped drawstring bottoms, and then, oh, so slowly, off came the tee shirt top.

Her breasts had always driven him crazy. They were more than a generous handful, with big, rosy nipples that responded to the slightest sensation. Like now. Even though he hadn't even begun touching her, he could see their nubs, stiff with arousal, as she drew closer to the bed. He knew that if he put his hand where it wanted to go, over the little garter briefs, he would feel her honeyed moistness through the thin cotton, telling him that she wanted him as much as he wanted her.

She sat next to him on the bed and he pulled her down, rolling her to her side so that he could position himself over her, all rock-hard, towering male strength. His kiss was like a release and he lost himself in it, covering her mouth with what started as a lazy exploration but rapidly turned into a blazing assault. She was sweetly, wildly irresistible, and he groaned as their tongues entwined. He felt as uncontrolled now as he had the first time he had ever touched her.

As he brought his questing mouth to her neck, she closed her eyes on a whimper and arched back.

'I've reached heaven,' Alessandro groaned. He fanned out his hands under her breasts, pushing them up, getting them ready for his mouth as he administered his attentions further down, along her shoulderblades and over the gentle pale slopes under which he could feel the rapid beating of her heart.

Unable to stand the exquisite torture, Megan brought his head to her nipples and half opened her eyes to watch as he began suckling on first one then the other, dividing his attention so that neither was spared the abrasion of his tongue as he laved them, or the delicate nipping of his teeth as he drew them deep into his mouth.

Her legs were spread as he straddled her, and his flat, hard stomach rubbed against her, sending her into a giddy, wild response that threatened to have her reaching orgasm when she wanted so badly to wait.

It was almost a blessed relief when he raised himself slightly, as though fully aware of how close she was to the edge. But the relief lasted barely a second as he left her breasts and began to work his way downwards.

His hands slid to her waist.

She had never been much of a believer in working out or going to the gym, but for all that her body had never seemed to need any such attentions. She was soft and feminine where she should be soft and feminine. A man could drown in the glory of her full breasts, and her waist was small, but not so slender that he could feel any protruding hipbones. Just small and soft and rounded, and Alessandro couldn't quite believe how he had managed the past seven years without her body.

He was so much taller and bigger than her, and yet they had always fitted perfectly together.

In comparison, the tall, leggy women he had endeavoured to replace her with now seemed like stiff, unyielding mannequins.

He lifted himself up for a few seconds to gaze at her flushed face, and when she looked back at him, he said roughly, 'Enjoying yourself, my darling?'

'You are *so* smug, Alessandro,' she said, and smiled lazily back.

'I like you being hot for me…' Unbidden came the agonising thought that she might have been equally hot for the other men she had slept with. Sure, they had been losers, or else one of them would still have been on the scene, but still…

Alessandro had never felt a second's worth of jealousy when it had come to any of the other women in his life, but the full weight of it slammed into him now, like a rampaging monster.

He didn't like it, and he steadied himself by remembering that this was simply something of the moment for both of them—sex to be enjoyed without the hassle of commitment. After all, look where his last step to commitment had led him. He would enjoy her, because in some undefined way this was something he had been waiting for. Her eager, pliant body writhing and squirming under his.

He would give her the best sex she had ever had.

He placed his hand between her legs and rubbed. Her soft moans were like music. Then, easing his body back down, he heard the soft moans become more urgent, and felt her body buck against him as he slid his tongue along into her, feeling out her small, sensitive bud. She tasted like honeyed dew, and weirdly it was as though the remembered taste had survived somewhere in his memory bank, waiting for just this moment to come rushing back to him.

He raised his eyes. She was arched back, and her breasts

were bouncing as she moved under him. Her nipples stood up, erect tips standing to attention.

He needed her right now, but he had come unprepared. With a groan of frustration, he asked her whether she was on contraception, and was almost disappointed to be told that she was.

He didn't want any accidents—of course he didn't! But neither did he want this ferocious jealousy at the thought that she might have been readying herself for another man.

It wasn't going to do. She had talked to him about not getting involved. Hell, he *wanted* her involved. He *wanted* her to belong utterly and entirely to *him*. He didn't want her thinking of anyone else. With supreme confidence, he knew that, as always, what he wanted he would get.

CHAPTER SIX

MEGAN propped herself up on her elbows and watched him. He made a great sleeper. He didn't snore, and he didn't thrash around the bed the way she did, so that in the morning the bedsheets were all over the place and at least one bit of her body was hanging over the edge, however big the bed happened to be.

And his was a big bed. Much bigger than her double bed. Big enough, in fact, to throw a party on it.

She sighed, slipped out from under the covers and headed for his bathroom. After nearly three weeks she was familiar with the layout of his house. She wasn't sure whether that was a good development or not.

She had had ample warning from Charlotte. *Have sex in haste*, she had been told, *and repent at leisure*. Even though Megan had told her repeatedly that it was all just about the sex, so there would be nothing to repent over *at leisure*.

What she had tactfully omitted to mention was that small sprig of hope which seemed to have taken root inside her, burrowing in between all her good intentions, finding the little crack where resolution met control and growing every day.

At the back of her mind was the notion that this time they were both different. She was older, and hopefully a little wiser. He had fulfilled his ambitions and maybe, just maybe, was ready for a proper relationship. It wasn't as though she was now standing in the way of him and his dream of conquering the world! He had already conquered it!

And then there was the business of Victoria. Hadn't he tried the path of finding the 'perfect woman' and come up short? Hadn't he told her that the perfect woman had not proved as satisfying as the *imperfect* one?

Maybe not in so many words, but Megan's fertile mind had busily read between the lines, and now…

Now she looked at her reflection in the mirror and sighed again.

'What are you doing in there?'

Megan started. She lived in daily fear that he would somehow read the thoughts in her head. It was one thing thinking the impossible. It was another thing should that weakness be exposed. Would he run a mile? In her crazy daydreams he wouldn't, but daydreams were a far cry from reality, and she was still managing to preserve a healthy scepticism—at least on the outside.

She peered round the door. Alessandro was now sitting up, sprawled amid ivory sheets, the purest of Egyptian cotton. 'I'm going to have a shower,' she told him. 'And then I'm heading home.'

'It's Saturday. Why are you heading home?'

He frowned. Three weeks ago he had considered it a pretty safe bet that she would be running at his beck and call the minute they were lovers. Indeed, Alessandro had taken that as a given. He had also thought long and hard about *why* he still wanted her and had come to the conclusion that it was because, as he had told her, she was his unfinished business. He had broken off their relationship because of circumstances, and of course had been right to do so, but sexually she was without compare, and he needed to *have* her before she cleared his system, so to speak. It made sense.

Unfortunately, whilst they were as rampant as teenagers and the sex was as satisfying as he had ever experienced, he wasn't *reaching* her. They met only on predetermined days, and on the one occasion when a meeting had taken him out of the country, she had smilingly but firmly refused to reorganise her calendar for the following evening. What, he had thought, could be so important in her life that she couldn't shuffle a few things about?

But when they *did* meet he had to admit that he was never disappointed. The sex was everything he could have wanted. It was familiar, and yet blazingly new at the same time. But there was always a part of her that she seemed to be holding back. And, call it a challenge to his male ego, he was determined to reach that part and scoop it out.

'Well?' He tried to pose it as a light question, but the demand was there, just under the surface. 'What's so important that you have to fly off at the break of dawn on a Saturday morning?'

'It's not the break of dawn. It's after ten.'

'That's quibbling over detail.' He patted the side of the bed invitingly. 'Come back to bed and we'll do something.'

'You're insatiable!' Megan laughed. 'I'm beginning to feel like a sex slave!'

'Not precisely what I was thinking of, but are you saying that you don't like the role?'

'I'm saying that even sex slaves need showers.' She looked at his bronzed body, entwined among the sheets, and itched to leap back into bed with him, to spend the whole day wrapped up in his arms, making love until they were too tired to move. When night fell maybe they would stir themselves, grab a takeout, settle in front of the television and watch one of those reality TV shows which he had always hated. Like a normal couple.

This was the forbidden hope and longing which she knew, in her saner moments, she had to fight, but now she compromised. 'We could always have a shower *together*.'

'Tempting…' He slashed a smile and swung out of the bed, as lithe and graceful as a panther.

Megan turned away, already warm at the thought of his hands on her.

'But before we turn on the water…'

Alessandro caught her from behind. In front of the floor-to-ceiling mirror, she watched his big, naked body behind hers. For a second their eyes met and tangled in the reflection. She watched his hand push up under her pyjama top, slowly kneading her heavy breasts. She could see the drowsy flush on her cheeks as he tugged her nipples between his fingers, and when he removed the top the person she was looking at was breathing quickly, chest rising and falling, her nipples turning deep pink as he continued to play with them.

The person in the mirror was not someone in control. She was in the grip of a passion too big for her. But Megan couldn't tear her eyes away from herself, watching as he continued playing with her, teasing her throbbing nipples with his fingers as he leaned down to nip and caress her neck with his mouth.

When he stopped paying attention to her breasts, leaving them full and aching, it was to hook his fingers in the elasticated waistband of her pyjama bottoms and run them delicately under the cotton against her skin—before driving his hand down between her thighs where he, oh, so slowly began to administer his full attention, rubbing the sensitised area with his hand while two fingers deliberately sought out her clitoris, tickling it until she wanted to pass out from the pleasure.

She made a motion to stop him before he took her to a point from which there would be no return, but Alessandro wasn't interested in having his own needs fulfilled. Not yet. No, he wanted to look in that mirror and watch her melt against him. He wanted to see the surrender in her eyes as he brought her to a climax.

He gave a grunt of satisfaction as the hand that had been trying to brush his away fell to her side and she curved back into him, her body twisting as he continued to press faster and harder, until she could no longer help the shuddering release that came in uncontrollable waves, leaving her spent against his hard chest.

If he hadn't been behind her, holding her, Alessandro was sure that she would have sunk to the ground from the power of her orgasm. She had cried out, and at that point had looked beautiful and flushed and helplessly in his control. And that had been immensely satisfying.

She curved round into him and he held her against him, his fingers tangled in her hair.

Gradually he could feel her breathing return to normal, and she laughed a little shamefacedly.

'I didn't want that to happen,' she protested, tilting her face up to his.

'I know,' Alessandro drawled. 'But I did. I wanted to feel you tremble against me as I brought you to fulfilment….'

'It was selfish. Sex is a two-way street.' She reached down and felt the hardness of him pressed against her. 'And don't you think that I'm going to let you get away that easily, mister.' She laughed again—a deep, throaty laugh. 'My turn now….'

But he obviously had more control than she did, because although she lavished as much attention on his arousal as he had on hers, he pulled her onto him and drove deep into her, his head thrown back and his eyes closed as he shuddered to his own climax, bringing her to another.

'I *really* think I need a shower now,' Megan said, when they were finally disentangled from each other. Her body was still tingling all over.

He had a huge wetroom, and it felt strangely natural to have her shower and wash her hair while he stood at the slate basin and shaved. They had fallen into a routine of seeing each other two nights a week. On a Wednesday and a Friday. She only ever stayed over on a Friday, and would leave bright and early on the Saturday morning. Sometimes they would have breakfast together. His chef always kept the fridge laden with delicacies. But she would always make sure that she was out of his house at a reasonable time. Hope might be there, and it might very well spring eternal, but there was no way that she was going to let herself get lulled into a false sense of security. At least not to the point where she would *do* anything about it.

'So…' He was wiping his face on one of the fluffy towels as he turned to face her. 'You never say why you have to rush off. Busy day ahead? Books to mark? Nails to paint? You can't tell me that there's hair to be washed, because you've already done that.'

Megan stepped out of the shower room and looked at him as he lounged indolently against the wide plate of marble that encased the slate washbasin. He had slung a towel around his waist and it hung low, a casual covering that paid token lip service to modesty.

'I always have books to mark. It's a never-ending exercise. Today it's English, and I'm expecting some fabulous stories from Year Four.'

'In other words you are rushing back for no good reason?'

Megan didn't say anything, because this was unfamiliar territory. She had laid down her ground rules and so far he had obeyed them. Sex without involvement. How was she supposed to cling to those ground rules if he started trying to break them?

'Marking books is a very good reason,' she began valiantly. 'I know you probably think that my job isn't as hard as yours—'

'That's not what I meant.' He strolled towards the shower, turned it on and said, casually, 'Don't even think about leaving until we're done with this conversation.'

'Conversation? I thought we were exchanging information about the day ahead.'

Alessandro heard her but chose not to reply, even though he was aware of her dithering by the misted glass.

He was going to take his time, and then—well, it was open to debate whether she would be scuttling off to her house in pursuit of marking 'fabulous stories from Year Four'. He had other plans in mind. Plans which he hadn't had a week ago, when their non-involvement relationship had still seemed a pretty good idea—especially on the back of Victoria.

Megan wasn't in the bedroom when he finally made it out of the bathroom, but she was waiting for him in the kitchen, sitting demurely at the kitchen table, warming her hands around a mug of coffee. Her rucksack was on the ground by her feet and her shoes were on. She was ready and prepared for a swift exit.

He scowled. 'Breakfast?'

Megan shook her head and finished what was left of the coffee in her cup. 'Must dash.'

Alessandro gritted his teeth as he poured himself coffee from the glass jug on the counter. He forced himself to smile. If she was so damned eager to leave, then snarling at her was only going to hasten her departure.

'I've been invited to a company do this evening,' he said conversationally, tugging out a chair with his foot and sitting to face her. 'Theatre and dinner.'

'Oh? That sounds nice. Anything interesting?'

He gave the name of a play which had only just hit the West End. Tickets were like gold dust.

'Lucky you.' Megan sighed. 'I'd love to see that, but the waiting list is probably ten years long. Still, it'll give me time to save up. Have you any idea how much theatre tickets cost?'

'No idea.'

'Well, an arm and a leg.' She stood up and glanced at her watch as she did a mental checklist in her head, to make sure that she had packed up all the stuff she had brought over. She was careful never to leave anything at his house. It was easy to be lazy, and that was a road she had travelled down before.

She had reached 'toothbrush'—*tick*—when he interrupted.

'I'm glad you're keen to see that play, because I need a partner and I'm inviting you to come along with me.'

Alessandro could tell immediately that she was appalled by the idea. First off there was her lack of response, and then her face fell. He could snap his fingers and have any woman he wanted leaping at the invitation, but here he was, confronted by the woman he was sleeping with—a woman who, seven years ago, would have squealed with delight at the offer—and she looked as though she was calculating what phony excuse she could dredge up by way of refusal.

'I…I can't.'

'And why would that be, Megan?' he asked with heavy sarcasm. 'Because your social diary is so jam-packed with exciting events that you can't possibly cancel?'

'Because it's not a good idea,' she told him bluntly. She sat back down and looked at him, cupping her chin in her hand.

'And why,' Alessandro asked with laboured patience, 'isn't it a good idea?'

'Because that's not what this deal is all about.'

He clenched his jaw and shoved himself away from the table. 'This so-called *deal* is beginning to get on my nerves,' he said harshly. 'I can't slot my sex life into a diary like a business appointment, and forget about it on the days we don't meet. It's unnatural.'

'It's necessary.'

'Are you telling me that I don't cross your mind on the days when we don't meet?' he demanded. 'If that's the case, then why are we *having* this relationship?'

'It's not a relationship!'

'No? Then tell me what it is.'

'We're attracted to each other and we're…following that attraction…' Yes, she had laid down the rules, but it still felt awful—*cheap* somehow—to refer to what they had as *just sex*. Furthermore, it was a lie. She thought about him *a lot*—analysed what they had over and over again. Did she mean anything to him? Was it really all about the sex for him and nothing else? Now he was telling her that it *was* more than just falling into bed and having fun twice a week. He was branching out from their arrangement. And while she didn't want to go down any slippery slopes, the little hope thing was rearing its head once again, teasing her with scenarios she knew were wrong.

Or were they?

'And would that be like dogs in heat?'

'I don't want you intruding into my life, Alessandro. You seem to have conveniently forgotten that I've been there before. I would have done anything for you back then.'

This, he recognised, was the sound of her raising the stakes, and it was reflected in the determined expression on her face. Take her on board in a full relationship, wherever that might lead, or else they kept what they had in boxes which were brought out on specific days and returned to their shelves as soon as the allotted time was over.

He could, of course, tell her that if the fairy-tale ending was what she was after then it was a promise too far. He could tell her that he had tried the total commitment thing with Victoria. It had crashed and burned, despite the fact that they were so utterly compatible in every way on paper, so there was no hope of it coming to anything with a woman who, theoretically, was the diametric opposite of him. But did he really want to do that? He was enjoying what they had, and when he thought about it it *wasn't* just the mind-blowing sex. Why bring it all to an abrupt end and be left with that sour taste of unfinished business all over again?

That made no sense, and Alessandro prided himself on being someone who was coolly and unequivocally practical.

'I'm not asking you to do anything for me,' he drawled, although the concept was enticing. 'But I'm not prepared to carry on a situation that involves us meeting up like thieves in the night and snatching a few minutes of passion before we slink back to our separate hideaways. I bet you haven't told anyone about us.'

'Charlotte knows.'

'And would that be only because you share a house with her, so it would be virtually impossible to conduct any *situation* without her finding out?' Her silence gave him the answer and he leaned towards her. 'I want more of you, Megan. Why don't we give what we have a chance? See where it leads and stop consigning it to some kind of artificial timetable?'

If she wanted to raise the stakes, then he was willing to go along for the ride.

Megan swallowed. She wanted to tell him that she would need a little time to think it through—that way she could maintain her control—but the way he was looking at her, his dark eyes steady and utterly, utterly mesmeric....

And wasn't this what she had secretly hoped for? That he would begin to consider a proper relationship with her? One that might actually stand a chance of going somewhere? She felt her heart begin to beat quickly. This was a step forwards for them, and, while she would take nothing for granted, she could either agree to relax her rigid timetable or else accept a *situation*, as he had put it, which would eventually end up being stifled by her self-imposed straitjacket.

The fact that he wanted to introduce her to some of his colleagues was also a big plus, because it indicated that at least he wasn't ashamed of her—which was what she had felt seven years ago, when he had dumped her. Ashamed of the girl who had it in her to pop out of a birthday cake in front of his Very Important Business Opportunities, as she had afterwards referred to the pinstriped trio whose meeting she had so rudely gatecrashed.

'When you say that we could give this *a chance*,' she prodded, 'what exactly do you mean?'

Put on the spot, Alessandro refused to concede further ground. 'Do you want to come or not?'

'I'm honestly not sure if I have anything suitable to wear....'

'Which is why I am suggesting we go shopping.'

'Go shopping?'

'It's something people tend to do now and again. Women seem to fall victim to the trend more often than men.'

'I know what shopping is, Alessandro. I just can't imagine it's the sort of thing *you* would enjoy doing on a Saturday.'

Megan savoured this further indication of advancement in their relationship. Hope was shooting up inside her like the proverbial beanstalk from the fairy story.

'It's not how I usually pass my time on a Saturday,' he agreed, 'but needs must.'

'You mean, you don't trust me to buy my own clothes?'

'I mean, I intend to buy whatever you need *for* you. If I tell you to go shopping with my credit card, you'll spend the next five hours arguing why you won't. Don't even think of it, Megan,' he said, seeing her open her mouth as this new thought dawned on her. 'I'm paying because you'll be coming to something at my request. You can wear whatever you want— bearing in mind that there's no green-and-red dress code....'

'Well...I *guess* I'm not doing anything much tonight....'

'Good.' He stood up, his mouth curving into a smile of triumph. 'Then let's go. You can leave that rucksack thing of yours here. No point going back to your house to change. You can come back here. We leave at six.'

Like someone suddenly finding that a gentle fairground ride was turning out to be a roller coaster stomach-churner, Megan was vaguely aware of a certain amount of manipulation. But when she tried to follow through with that suspicion, she found that all she could actually think about was the fact that this was the first really *normal* thing they had done since they had locked themselves away in their little bubble of sexual gratification.

She looked at the rucksack lying on the ground, as if it might just deliver the answer to the question she was asking herself—which was whether she should open this door or not. But she knew that she would. She had fought to be sensible, but the fact that he had broken off his engagement with Victoria *because of her*, because of the attraction he still felt to *her*, must mean something. That was the steady drip, drip, drip continually eroding her good intentions.

'We'll start at Selfridges, shall we?' Alessandro said, before she had a chance to change her mind. Suddenly it was very important that she yield to what he wanted. 'Unless you have somewhere else in mind?'

'I guess I could do Selfridges....'

Several hours later and Megan had discovered that she could do a great deal more than Selfridges. Shopping with a wealthy

Alessandro was a completely different affair from shopping with a broke Alessandro, and although she refused to allow him to buy her anything that wasn't going to be worn that evening to the theatre, she still found herself the owner of a new pair of shoes, a fabulous dress, jewellery which she insisted she would wear just the once and then give back to him—because she couldn't possibly accept a gift with that kind of price tag—a coat of the warmest, softest cashmere, and a selection of make up which she would never have been able to afford in a million years.

Over lunch, she made sure to stress her returns policy. 'That jewellery is ridiculous, Alessandro,' she said, toying with a fat, juicy prawn. 'Anyway, where on earth would I ever wear it after tonight? And the coat... Well, it's beautiful, but it just doesn't feel right to accept stuff from you.'

Alessandro shrugged and declined to mention that he was accustomed to spending far, far more on the women he had dated in the past—women who had never had any qualms about accepting the tremendously expensive gifts that had been lavished upon them. Somehow he didn't think that the observation would have gone down too well. He also declined to tell her that this was the first time he had ever *physically* gone shopping with any woman. It was a task which he preferred to leave to his personal assistant. And he decided to keep to himself the fact that he had actually enjoyed the expedition—enjoyed watching her parade in a selection of outfits for him to see, enjoyed seeing the way her eyes opened wide at the sheer beauty of some of the dresses. It had all given him a kick.

'You can give it all back if it makes you feel better,' he told her 'But if you do it'll all end up stuffed at the back of a wardrobe somewhere. I, personally, have no use for women's clothing or jewellery.'

Megan looked at him. This was a different animal from the one she had known. Urban, sophisticated, blasé about the things money could buy—things that were well beyond the reach of most ordinary mortals. From out of nowhere came the uneasy thought that she was now out of his league even more than she had been seven years ago. At least then they had been broke together.

But she wasn't going to think about that. She was going to enjoy the rest of the day and the evening ahead. So she smiled and didn't say anything—but the prawns no longer looked quite as appetising as they had.

'Who's going to be at the theatre tonight?' She changed the subject and closed her knife and fork conclusively on the remaining sad prawns on her plate. 'Anyone exciting?'

'Aside from me?' Alessandro grinned at her.

'Your ego's showing again,' she teased, relaxing after that brief spell of unwelcome thought. 'Careful, Alessandro. If it gets any bigger then you won't be able to get through the doors to the theatre.'

'Well, my darling, you know you need only concern yourself with me.'

'But what if there's a really fantastic-looking guy there?'

'Are you telling me that you're on the lookout for another man?'

There was a chill note of warning in his voice.

'I'm not your property, Alessandro.'

'When it comes to my women, I don't do sharing.'

'Well, I would never dream of sleeping around, and I'm insulted that you would think that of me.' She looked at him coldly, and eventually he gave her a conciliatory smile.

'You're right—and it's good that we understand one another.'

He called for the bill and she watched as he left a wad of cash, which included a generous tip for the waitress. If there was one thing she couldn't accuse him of being it was stingy, but it still took a little while for the slightly sour end of their shopping day to disappear, and it really wasn't until she was standing in front of the mirror at a little before six that her spirits were once more where they should be.

With the whole outfit put together—the classic jewellery round her neck, the perilously high shoes adding a further four inches to her frame, the dress which clung in all the right places—she felt like a million dollars, and she felt even better when she saw the expression in his eyes as he stood watching her descend the staircase.

'Maybe,' he growled, taking her in his arms, 'we should just keep the taxi waiting a few minutes.'

Megan laughed throatily and touched the extravagant string of diamonds at her neck. 'I'm not missing a minute of this play, Alessandro Caretti!'

'Are you telling me that I take second place in your life to a bunch of actors on a stage?'

'I'm afraid so.' She sighed and shook her head regretfully.

'You know…' he kissed her neck, which she wished he hadn't because now her body was responding, opening up like a flower for him '…you'll have to make up for that terrible insult later….'

'Oh? Will I, really?'

Of course he was expecting her to spend the night at his house! It would be ludicrous to drive all the way out to her place from the West End at some silly time of night! The roller-coaster ride seemed to be picking up speed.

'Yes,' Alessandro told her gravely, 'you will. And if you don't mind, I'll just check to make sure that you're getting in the mood….'

He slid his hand under her dress, up along her thigh, and felt the stirrings of arousal as his finger slipped underneath the scrap of silk he hadn't been able to stop thinking about ever since they'd purchased it in the lingerie department earlier that day. If the taxi hadn't been there he would have yanked up that dress and taken her right there in the hall. He had never been in the grip of such uncontrollable passion in his life before. He removed his hand and smoothed down the dress with an audible sigh of regret.

When he looked at her, her face was flushed, her breathing uneven.

'Stop that,' he said unsteadily, and Megan gathered herself sufficiently to answer.

'Stop what?'

'Looking so damned sexy. An outing to the theatre doesn't stand a chance when your mouth is begging to be kissed… along with every other part of your body….'

His cellphone beeped, and he picked up the call from the taxi driver, telling them that he was waiting outside. He should, he thought, have handed the job to his own driver, but a family illness had seen him off for the week. Now he would have to sit through the entire evening watching a musical in which he had no particular interest, making polite conversation to a bunch of people in whom he had only marginally more interest, when he knew that his woman was right there next to him, hot and eager and desperate to be kissed all over. Worse, they would have to wait at the mercy of a black cab to bring them back to the house late.

'Duty calls,' he said sourly, and Megan tiptoed to give him a fluttery kiss on his mouth—because it gave her a heady feeling of power to have him looking like that. As though she was the only woman in the world, as though he wanted to ravish her senseless on the wooden floor of his hall.

'It's going to be fun.'

'I loathe musicals.'

'This is going to be brilliant,' Megan assured him as he helped her on with the coat. 'The lead singer was recruited on a reality television show.'

'And I loathe reality television shows even more. So put those two things together and I have no idea why I agreed to go in the first place.' He folded her against him as they walked out to the taxi. 'Just as well I shall have something to look forward to when we get back….'

But Megan was excited. It had been ages since she had last been to the theatre. It also made a nice change to be going out. Between seeing Alessandro and doing the routine business of her work, a lot of her extra-curricular hobbies had gone by the wayside. Her football games, which were on a Wednesday, had been ditched in favour of him. Thinking about it, so had a number of her friends outside work—including Robbie, whom she hadn't seen since New Year's Eve.

She frowned and wondered at how quickly her spare time was being eaten away.

She would have to do something about that—give Robbie a call in the week, see what he had been up to, maybe arrange to meet him for a drink.

Alessandro hadn't mentioned the football coach for a while, so hopefully he wouldn't mind her meeting him. Good friends should never be dropped in favour of a relationship, however preoccupying that relationship might be.

He also never spoke of Victoria, and all attempts to get him on the subject had been stillborn. It was as if she had never existed.

She looked at him in the darkness of the cab. Aside from the standard white shirt, he was in black. Black trousers, black jacket, black coat. He looked dangerous, but then he turned to her, smiled, and pulled her towards him, and Megan settled in the crook of his arm with a contented sigh.

'Are you glad I persuaded you to come with me tonight?' he asked softly, and after a moment's hesitation Megan nodded—because what could be better than this? 'And, in case I haven't told you, you look amazing.'

'Is it the sort of thing Victoria would have worn?' The words had left her mouth before she could hold them back, and she could feel Alessandro stiffen next to her.

'It is immaterial what Victoria would have worn or not worn. Don't compare yourself to her. I don't.'

Megan sank closer against him with a contented sound. 'I know, and you don't realise how much that means to me, Alessandro. That you don't compare us. That you broke off your engagement because of me.'

She raised her head to look at him, but he was staring through the window, and in the darkness of the taxi she couldn't make out the expression on his face.

CHAPTER SEVEN

MEGAN had expected the others in their party to be replicas of the pinstriped trio, but in fact, she was pleasantly surprised to find that they were neither old nor boring. One of the women, Melissa, was radiantly pregnant, and was keenly interested to hear everything about the school at which Megan taught—because, as she explained earnestly, although her baby was still only a seven-month bump, names had to be put on registers for private schools as early as possible. Places were so oversubscribed in certain boroughs.

'Ideally, I'd like to move to the country,' she confided, as they were swept along in the crowd to their seats. 'But apparently that's not where the money is. At least not the banking money.'

'I'm going to move back to the country,' Megan said wistfully. 'As soon as I've got enough experience at my school. Maybe in a couple of years' time. Somewhere green and pleasant, as they say. Lots of open fields and trees and rabbits.'

'I don't see Alessandro feeling comfortable around fields and trees and rabbits,' Melissa said, one hand on her stomach.

'Oh, I know! He's definitely a city kind of guy! He enjoys the fast pace, and the cut-throat, watch-out-for-the-knife-in-the-back kind of lifestyle….'

Alessandro, who was right behind her, could hear every

word—even though he was apparently keenly tuned in to a conversation about the stockmarket—and he wasn't sure whether he liked the fact that Megan was discussing a future without him in it. Of course what they had would fizzle out in due course…they were both dealing with the process of successful closure of a relationship. The intensely gratifying sex would inevitably become mundane, at which point they would bid each other goodbye with a little sigh of relief that they were over one another at last. But shouldn't *he* be the one to decide when that point in time came?

'Escape back to the country…?' he murmured, as soon as they were seated, conveniently at the very end of their row.

Megan looked at him with surprise. 'Were you eavesdropping on my conversation?' she asked lightly.

'I prefer to call it taking a healthy interest in what's happening around me. You never told me that you were planning to bolt back to the countryside. Back up to Scotland?'

'You make it sound as though I've already bought the rail ticket and packed my bags. And, no, I don't think I'll be moving back to Scotland any time soon. You could say I've become accustomed to the tropical weather down south.'

Megan watched, entranced, at the people moving between the seats, programmes in their hands. She had forgotten how exciting the atmosphere in a theatre could be—the feeling of pleasant anticipation that hung in the air just before the curtain was raised, the orchestra at the front, trying out a few bars, getting the note just right for when they launched into the first number.

'But London doesn't suit you…' Alessandro murmured.

'It suits me at the moment. But, no, I can't see myself staying here to live for ever.'

'Because it suits people like me? People who enjoy the jungle warfare of the business world?'

Megan looked sideways at the man sitting next to her. In

his dark suit and trademark white shirt, with his gold watch peeping from under the cuffs of the shirt and his dark hair slicked back and curling, slightly too long, against his collar, he should have been just another very rich, very well-dressed, above averagely good-looking businessman. But there was something raw and untamed lurking just beneath the urbane, sophisticated exterior—something that made heads swing round and made people falter in their footsteps. *Jungle warfare?* He couldn't have chosen a better metaphor.

'Guess so,' she told him. 'Don't tell me you don't *enjoy* the fast pace of living in London! You'd go nuts if you were stuck out in the countryside with nothing better to do than laze around watching nature.'

Megan thought how nice it would be just to take time out of the low-level stress that came from being involved with a man when she knew that he would break her heart—just as he had done the first time round. This was what it had been like seven years ago. Fast, furious, sizzling excitement. It had been wild and heady, but it hadn't been relaxing then and it wasn't relaxing now. Her only relaxation came from her private daydreams, in which she constructed a happy ending based on nothing more substantial than the fact that he was with her now and it was his conscious choice.

She hadn't, until right now, even considered the possibility of moving out to the countryside. Melissa had raised the subject and she had replied out of politeness. But, thinking about it, it was beginning to seem more appealing by the second.

She had spent the day on cloud nine, shopping with Alessandro, fighting hard to maintain a cool, detached exterior while her heart had been racing. And just at the moment she was keenly and painfully aware of him next to her, leaning into her so that he could whisper into her ear. His warm breath against her neck made every nerve-ending in her body tingle. Was all of that *desirable*? Moreover, she seemed to have no control over what he *did* to her. Her body and her mind seemed to lose the ability to function normally the minute he was around. Was that a *good* way to be?

'But me,' she said, not looking at him and warming to the idea of a life that wasn't lived in a permanent state of nervous anticipation, 'I'd love the countryside. I'd love to have a little cottage with clambering roses on a white picket fence, and a milkman delivering milk to the door every day. I could teach at a small village school. Maybe,' she elaborated wistfully, 'I would take up knitting.'

Alessandro gave a burst of laughter that had a few eyes turning in their direction. A few, having seen him, lingered a little longer than was necessary.

'I thought you'd already done the rural school fantasy. And *knitting*? You?'

'It's a possibility!' Megan snapped in a low, irritated voice.

'I think your personality might get in the way of such a placid pastime.' Alessandro smirked, thinking of her dressed in that wisp of red and green, with one impractical red shoe sailing through the air. 'I'm not sure if a woman who enjoys running around a muddy football pitch would be content to spend two months in front of a television, knitting a scarf. Seven years ago your dream was to go hang-gliding. How does *that* equate with *knitting*?'

'Okay, maybe not *knitting*,' she said. 'Maybe *rambling*, or…or…'

'Or…or…*bird-watching*…or…or…*embroidery*…or…or… Get a grip, Megan. The picket fence and the clambering roses might sound fine in theory, but in reality you'd be bored stiff. Isn't that why you came down to London? To escape a serious case of open-field syndrome?'

'Maybe now that I've tried the big-city life I'm ready to get back to my *open-field syndrome*!'

'You might just find that's easier said than done.'

Alessandro didn't know why he was getting hot under the collar at Megan's innocent conversation, but it gnawed away at him throughout the whole of the first half of the musical.

He was vaguely aware of dutifully clapping in all the right places—just as he was vaguely aware that the woman next to him was totally absorbed in what was happening on the stage. But he was largely preoccupied with the disturbing suspicion that *he* wanted to be the one calling all the shots. Was that just his male ego talking? From the lofty heights of someone who was used to giving orders and having them obeyed without question, Alessandro had piously thought that he was *not* one of those guys who got off on being always in control.

By the time intermission rolled around, he was in the grip of a pretty foul mood, made more foul by Megan's bubbly chatter and her insistence on getting his thoughts on what he had seen so far. Wasn't the choreography brilliant? Wasn't the singing fantastic? Wasn't that little kid just *so* adorable?

Alessandro was non-committal as they headed for the bar, where drinks had been pre-ordered.

'Not too many musicals in the countryside these days,' was what he heard himself saying. 'Although probably quite a few barn dances.'

'What's it to you whether I bury myself in the countryside to pursue my hobby of knitting and going to barn dances?' Megan asked tartly.

Ahead of them, the other members of their party had become submerged in the chaos of the bar.

This whole stupid conversation seemed to have become a battle of wills, and Megan wasn't going to back down.

'Obviously not much,' Alessandro drawled darkly. 'You

can bury yourself wherever you want to. I merely felt compelled to point out the drawbacks to your master plan.'

'And thanks very much for that. But I'm a big girl now. I think I can work out how to live my life without your advice. In fact—' she furthered her cause for independence '—if you'll make my excuses to everyone, I'm going to join the queue for the Ladies'. I might not be back in time for my glass of wine.'

She wasn't one hundred per cent sure where the restrooms were, and nor did she really need to go, but she needed to put some distance between herself and Alessandro. This should have been a *fun* evening. Instead the fun bit was getting lost in an uncomfortable argument about nothing in particular. If, she thought furiously as she battled through the crowds like a fish swimming upstream, he hadn't wanted to bring her along to the theatre, then he should never have invited her. But he had asked her along and then proceeded to pick a row over her silly, purely hypothetical plan to move out to the country. Just because, she reasoned, he had to be the one whose opinions were always right.

Was she getting on his nerves? Was this his way of showing it?

She reached the restrooms to find the line of people as long as she had expected. Longer. And moving at a snail's pace. But at least it would give her the chance to get back her cheerful frame of mind, so that she could enjoy the second half of the musical.

She was miles away when a familiar voice said from behind, 'Megan? Is that you?'

Megan spun around to find Victoria standing right behind her, exquisite in a pale woollen, long-sleeved dress with a string of pearls around her neck. Her hair, for the first time since Megan had met her, fell in a neat, glossy bob to her shoulders.

'Victoria!'

'Isn't this a surprise? Who are you here with?'

The line was shuffling forwards very slowly. 'I'm with…' Megan hesitated, guiltily aware that Alessandro's name might be a depressing reminder to the other woman of her broken engagement. 'A few…friends. And you? You look tremendous, by the way. And Dominic, I gather, is still head over heels in love with football! I'm so glad about that.'

'So am I,' Victoria confided with a warm smile. 'And I have *you* to thank for that.'

Megan mumbled something in return.

'In fact, I have you to thank for a number of things. Look, are you absolutely desperate for the loo? We could just slope off and have a quiet chat before the second half begins. There are a few things I'd rather like to get off my chest.'

Megan swallowed hard and wished herself back to the bar—because arguing with Alessandro suddenly seemed more restful than hearing what Victoria had to say.

'Of course.' She resigned herself to the inevitable and followed Victoria, who seemed to know the layout of the theatre a lot better than she did. In fact, they managed to avoid the crowds altogether, and were shown by one of the ushers to a quiet side room just off the stage.

'Sometimes it's jolly convenient to have connections,' Victoria explained apologetically. 'My uncle is something of a bigwig in the field of theatre.' She tapped the side of her nose and gave a conspirational smile. 'A quiet word in the right ear and here we are. Far from the madding crowd.'

'I'm here with Alessandro!' Megan blurted out, taking the bull by the horns rather than waiting for the bull to come charging at her.

She walked over to one of the small flowered sofas and stood behind it, her hands resting on the upholstered back.

'Look, I really am so sorry that things didn't work out between the two of you, but I want you to know that the—'

'You're here with Alessandro? I'm *so* glad!'

'You're…what…?' Megan asked faintly.

'So awfully glad.' Victoria looked at her ruefully. 'I felt so dreadfully guilty at the way things ended between us.'

'You felt *dreadfully guilty*?' Her mind seemed to be getting a little clogged up, and now she was repeating language she never normally used! But there was a dull pink tinge to Victoria's face, and she did look very sheepish.

What, Megan wondered, was there for her to feel *sheepish* about? Alessandro had terminated the relationship, had broken off the engagement. Wasn't she entitled to feel a little hard done by?

'Why on earth would *you* feel guilty, Victoria?' she asked in genuine puzzlement.

'I never meant to meet Robbie! And I certainly never meant to—'

Robbie? Megan wondered what Robbie had to do with all of this. She felt as though she was in possession of a jigsaw puzzle, the key pieces of which were missing.

'Dominic absolutely adores him.'

'Good.' Megan tried to work out what was going on. 'It's nice,' she added vaguely, 'for a boy to have a role model, so to speak….'

'And I…' Victoria took her hand in a gesture that Megan suspected was heartfelt rather than customary. 'I felt so terribly awful about Alessandro…but Robbie…'

Pieces of the jigsaw were beginning to mesh together, and even though the picture wasn't as yet comprehensive Megan was slowly realising that she didn't like what she was seeing.

As if to confirm the suspicions forming at the back of her mind, she watched Victoria's face flush with happiness.

'I had to break off the engagement,' she confessed. 'Or rather the matter was taken out of my hands!' She laughed ruefully. 'Freudian slip, I'm afraid. I left my mobile phone at your Christmas party… Actually, I thought I had left it somewhere, put it down, but it turned out to have been in Alessandro's pocket all the while. He found out the worst possible way that Robbie…'

'Found out…?' Megan said in a dazed fashion. Her brain was frantically trying to keep pace with what was being said.

'Of course I never would have dreamt of doing anything!' Victoria exclaimed, misinterpreting the whiteness of Megan's face. 'But Robbie had been texting me…and I did realise that I found him…well…I was absolutely confounded…but…'

'So you told Alessandro?' Megan numbly asked for complete clarification.

'I had to. I couldn't possibly continue the relationship when there had been such a *sea change*, so to speak. You do understand, don't you?' Victoria asked anxiously. 'Of course Alessandro said that he was absolutely fine…' She smiled. 'But I can't tell you how marvellous it is to know that he's here…that you are with him… You *are* with him, aren't you? Darling, I *knew* there was something between you two… Perhaps in the end this is all a question of fate….'

She glanced at her watch and gave a little squeal of dismay.

'Robbie's going to be raging if he gets back to his seat and I'm not there!' She leapt to her feet. 'I've ordered him to get me an ice cream…if I don't rescue it, it will either be dripping down his hand or else he will have polished it off! You know men….'

No, Megan thought as she sprinted behind Victoria to find that the crowds had all returned to their seats for the second half of the play. No, she *didn't* know men. Not at all. She especially didn't know Alessandro.

Those little glimmers of hope that had darted in and out of her mind like fireflies, lighting up a future with promises which she knew would never be fulfilled but which had kept her busy with a little luxury wishful thinking, were now extinguished in a matter of seconds.

Alessandro hadn't broken off his engagement to Victoria *because of her*. He had been on the receiving end of a woman who had fallen in love with another man and had done the decent thing.

No *wonder* Robbie had not been in touch! She'd kept thinking that she should get in touch with him, but she had been so preoccupied with Alessandro that she had barely given anything else a second's thought. He had taken over her daily existence, just as he had seven years previously, even though she had given herself lots of stern lectures about maintaining detachment.

She thought back to the way she had nurtured her hope that this time things would be different between them, and was swamped by a feeling of disgust at her gullibility.

She didn't like to think how long she would have continued seeing him, weaving little dreams in her head about a perfect life with him. Fortunately Victoria had set her straight on that one.

I'm hurting now, Megan thought as she returned to her seat, forcing down the bitter sting of tears at the back of her throat. *But it's all for the best and time is a great healer.*

She could feel Alessandro turn to her in the darkness as she slipped back into her seat next to him, but she kept her head averted.

She didn't know how she managed to sit through the remainder of the play. The dancing which she had thought was so marvellous in the first half barely distracted her from her angry, humiliated, churning thoughts, and she fidgeted, keen to be rid of the intimacy of sitting next to him.

'What's the matter with you?' Alessandro murmured, conclusively sorting out her restless hands by anchoring his fingers around her wrist.

Megan immediately fell still. Only an hour before and she would have leant against him, hotly and wickedly anticipating another night spent in the same bed as him.

'Well?'

'Nothing. I'm just enjoying the play,' she muttered. After a couple of minutes she managed to extract her hand from his and place it on her lap.

There was a standing ovation for the performers, and while she stood up, she made sure to also be gathering her coat and busying herself with her handbag. The clothes which she had enjoyed buying with him now felt tainted on her.

It wouldn't take him long to figure out that something wasn't right. Alessandro was nothing if not adept at sensing nuance. But luckily he had no time to question her because he was caught up in the melee of everyone leaving the theatre. A meal out afterwards had been planned. There was no way on earth that Megan was going to go along.

As soon as they exited the theatre she turned to the assembled group and said, with an apologetic smile, 'I feel awful about doing this, but I'm going to have to cry off tonight's meal, I'm afraid.' She was aware of Alessandro, straight ahead of her and sandwiched between two of the men, looking at her sharply through narrowed eyes. 'Female problems.' She turned to Melissa who glowed with sympathy.

Female problems encompassed a gamut of irrefutable excuses, not one of which any man would ever question. It was an accepted fact that the mere mention of *female problems* sent most men diving for cover.

'Poor thing.' Alessandro moved forwards and took her arm in what could loosely be called a vice grip. 'And not a word to me about them. Such a martyr. But, darling, I couldn't possibly allow you to go back on your own when you're struggling with *female problems*.' He flashed his own apologetic smile all round. 'If you will excuse me? I must cut short this evening which has been so thoroughly enjoyable.'

'There's no need, Alessandro!' Her voice sounded high-pitched and panicked, and she toned it down with a belated smile. 'I just need to have an early night.'

'And I will make sure that you are safely delivered back to your bed.'

'How gallant,' one of the women said, before looking at her own portly husband with an indulgent grin. 'You need to take some lessons from Alessandro, Jamie. Remind me a bit that chivalry isn't dead.' She patted Megan kindly on her arm. 'Such a nuisance for you, my dear, but just so long as you've enjoyed the play. Stunning, wasn't it?'

Alessandro, Megan noticed miserably, kept his hand clamped round her arm as they said their goodbyes. Did he think that she might do a runner if he didn't?

She found herself in the back seat of a taxi while Alessandro gave orders for them to be taken back to his house.

'I want to go back to my own place.' Megan turned to him and edged away ever so slightly.

'You do realise how rude you've been?' He ignored her request and looked at her grimly.

'I'm sorry about that.'

'You don't look particularly sorry.' He raked his fingers through his hair. In the darkness, there was a dangerous glitter in his eyes that would have sent a shiver down her spine if she weren't feeling so *angry*. 'Let's just cut through the crap, Megan. If you've got *female problems,* then I'm the King of England. You were fine today when we were out, and you were perfectly well up until the second half. What the hell's going on?'

'I need to talk to you,' Megan said stiffly, 'and the back seat of a taxi isn't the place.' Nor was his house, for that matter, but there was no way he was going to drop her home, and anyway she had some of her possessions at his place, which she would have to collect.

Alessandro looked first at the distance she had put between them, at her hands which were balled into fists on her lap, and then at her profile as she stared out of the window.

Need to talk? Female problems?

His justified annoyance at her abrupt end to the evening did a rapid U-turn. She had said that she needed to talk to him—correction, that she needed to talk *privately*—and she had said it in a voice that had made him vaguely uneasy. Add to that the fact that she was sitting like an iceberg next to him, and he came up with the one explanation which made sense.

He didn't know how, but it was suddenly clear to him that she had managed to get pregnant. She had disappeared to the restrooms at the theatre, had remained there for an inordinately long time, and then had returned with a personality transplant. Had she taken some kind of testing kit to the loo? Maybe being in the company of Melissa had got her thinking about her menstrual cycle? Made her wonder if it had been as regular as it should have? Who knew? Alessandro wasn't a doctor, but he was pretty sure that he had hit jackpot.

He lapsed into a reflective silence of his own as he began to consider the possibilities of this unexpected event.

He had not considered his relationship with Megan to be a permanent one. She was an itch that he needed to scratch—a fever that roared through his system and needed curing once and for all. A pregnancy would change all that. He thought about becoming a father. Megan wasn't like Victoria. She would see parenthood as a full-time occupation. Broken nights, changing nappies, sterilising bottles—all of that would be, for her, a shared venture. His life would be turned on its head.

Alessandro looked at her. For someone who must be churning up inside, she appeared remarkably calm. In fact, for someone who was perfectly happy to be swept along on an emotional tide, she seemed to be handling the situation with a lot of *sang froid*.

The taxi pulled up outside his house.

'Okay,' he said, opening his front door and standing back to let her walk past him. 'You've had time to try and work out whatever speech you've got prepared...' Alessandro slammed the door behind him and stayed where he was, leaning against it and watching her. 'So what's this *talk* about? Anything to do with those *female problems* you mentioned, by any chance?'

On her way to the sitting room, Megan stopped in her tracks and turned to face him.

'What do you mean?'

'You know what I mean. I wasn't born yesterday, Megan. You're pregnant, aren't you?'

After the ensuing silence, during which Megan tried to gather her scattered wits and not burst into laughter at his wild, inaccurate deduction, Alessandro continued calmly.

'I don't know how it's happened, but it has, and now you're trying to work out how to break the news.'

'Oh, right. Is *that* what I'm doing? And how would you suggest I go about it?' Megan's voice was cool and level. He imagined she was *pregnant*? That, she thought, would have been one complication too far, and she was mightily relieved that she didn't have to deal with it.

Alessandro was a little unsettled by that response. Not a flicker of emotion had crossed her face. 'Just come right out and confess,' he advised. 'You can't skirt round a pregnancy.'

'And how will you react?' Megan tried to tear herself away from a pointless conversation about a non-existent situation. But it was tempting to buy time, and even more tempting to try and find out what he might have felt *had* he been confronted with a pregnant lover.

Part of her knew that she was just shoring up that little twig of hope, building herself a little fantasy that maybe, in a situation like that, he might suddenly be overwhelmed by need and love and race to her side in a supportive way. He wouldn't.

'It doesn't matter,' she told him in an icy voice. 'I'm not pregnant, so you can stop worrying.'

Surprisingly, Alessandro wasn't sure that he *had* been worrying. More contemplating jumping into unknown waters….

'Okay…' he said, moving towards her very slowly and watching her the way he might watch a domestic pet that had suddenly become dangerously unpredictable. 'So what is this all about, then?'

'It's about *us*, Alessandro.'

'What *about* us?'

'I've thought about this arrangement of ours and I've decided that the time has come to end it.' She thought bitterly of that other self—the one who had existed less than two hours ago, the one who had become caught up in all sorts of silly, reckless dreams. She folded her arms and stood her ground while he looked at her in perfect bemusement.

'You don't know what you're saying,' Alessandro told her amiably. 'Did you take a knock to your head when you went to the restroom at the theatre? Maybe you need to lie down?'

'I don't need to lie down. I need to go upstairs and get my stuff, then I'm leaving this house and I won't be coming back.'

The amiable smile dropped from Alessandro's face, but before he could pick her up on what she was saying—which made absolutely no sense whatsoever—she had turned her back to him and was running up the stairs.

After a second's hesitation he followed her, easily catching up with her and blocking the door to his bedroom.

'Just like that?' he ground out. 'You're leaving *just like that*? No explanation? Well, I refuse to allow it.'

'You *refuse to allow it*?' Megan gave a burst of mirthless laughter, but she was trembling.

'Yes, dammit!'

'You can do a lot of things, Alessandro, but you can't stop me walking out on you.'

'What's happened?'

'Nothing happened. I just wised up, that's all.'

'No, it damn well isn't all! I can read people, and you weren't planning on leaving me this morning, when we were out shopping! Nor were you planning to leave me when we were at the theatre—at least not until after the intermission. You disappeared for a while. What happened? Who did you talk to?'

Megan had not intended to go into details. When she had said goodbye to Victoria, she had been in a daze. The second half of the play, which she should have enjoyed but which in reality she would have been hard-pressed to remember, had given her time to try and collect her thoughts, and thought number one had been that she wasn't going to go down the post-mortem route. She was going to be cool and dignified and leave him to stew with unanswered questions.

He probably wouldn't stew for very long, but the thought of him stewing at all might well distract her from her misery at no longer being with him. She couldn't get out of her mind the thought that she had dug herself a hole, jumped in, and proceeded to cover herself with earth. All her crazy hopes had been based on a piece of fiction.

Of course now that she was actually facing his barrage of questions, and staring into those black, intense eyes in which she had happily lost herself, she no longer felt quite so content with a dignified exit.

She had never been able to master the art of being cool.

'Well?' Alessandro demanded. 'Are you just going to stand there, gaping like a goldfish?'

'Let me pass! I want to get my stuff!'

'Not until we've had some kind of conversation about this!'

'You always have to get your own way, don't you, Alessandro?' she responded in a shrill voice, which sent his temper levels up by a couple of notches.

'That's pretty much it,' he agreed. 'And the sooner you start realising that, the better for all concerned.'

'Okay. I'll tell you what you want to know.' She took a couple of deep breaths to calm herself. 'Guess who I bumped into when I was waiting in the queue for the toilet?'

'No idea. Why don't you enlighten me?'

'Your ex! Victoria. Remember her?'

'Of course I remember her,' Alessandro said warily. 'How is she?'

'Oh, she's doing just fine, now that you ask! Better than fine, in fact. Positively thriving.'

Alessandro waited.

'Aren't you going to ask me what we chatted about?'

'Why don't we go downstairs to finish this conversation?' he said in a grim voice. 'You said that you didn't want to talk in the taxi because it wasn't the right place. Well, getting hysterical on the landing isn't the right place for me.'

Megan wanted to tell him that it was the right place for *her*, because that way she might have asserted a little of her willpower, but in actual fact her legs felt wobbly, and while she knew that heading straight towards the question-and-answer session she had wanted to avoid was going to be undignified, collapsing outside his bedroom door because her legs were like jelly would have been even more undignified.

'Fine,' she said in the calmest voice she could muster. 'But once I'm done talking I collect my things and I leave this house for ever.'

CHAPTER EIGHT

ALESSANDRO watched Megan from across the unbridgeable width of the sitting room. She had adopted a defiant pose, perched on the ledge of the bay window. She hadn't removed her coat and she was huddled into it, even though the central heating was still on and the room was warm.

Too warm, in fact. He rid himself of his jacket and rolled the sleeves of his shirt to the elbows.

'Drink?' he asked, and when she shook her head, he shrugged and said, 'Well, I could do with one.'

Megan looked at him with mounting anger as he went across to one of the cupboards which slid noiselessly back to reveal a well-stocked bar.

The man was as cool as a cucumber! She had just threatened to leave him, to walk out of his house for good, and how was he reacting? As though nothing had been said! As though this was just another normal day at the ranch!

'You were saying…?' Alessandro turned back to her and sipped his whisky.

'I was saying that I bumped into Victoria, and she told me what happened between the two of you.' Megan drew in a deep breath and, taking her cue from him, banked down the emotion that was threatening to spiral out of control. Her voice was flat and calm. 'I was under the impression that *you* were responsible for the break-up, Alessandro.'

'Does it matter where the finger points? When it comes to the breakdown of a relationship there is nothing to be gained from apportioning blame.'

'Don't try and twist words,' Megan said bitterly. 'I was led to believe that you broke off your engagement because you wanted a relationship with *me*…'

'You believed what you wanted to believe,' Alessandro told her, his fury mounting at being called to account. He braced himself for the inevitable direction of the conversation.

'So you're not going to deny that Victoria was the one who decided to break off your engagement?'

The last pathetic shred of hope that he might at least try to disabuse her of Victoria's version of what had taken place shrivelled and died in the face of his continued silence.

'She told me about her mobile phone,' Megan continued in a hollow voice. Now that her decision to be cool and to walk away without explanation because he didn't deserve one had been abandoned, she felt driven to expose every little detail of her own foolishness. It was like picking away at a scab. It wouldn't remedy anything but it was still an unstoppable temptation.

And still there was nothing from him. He just stood there, taking small sips of his drink, seemingly at ease with the situation.

'You found out that Robbie had been in touch with her, and I guess before you could—I don't know—try and make her go down the *sensible* route, she decided that she wanted to throw caution to the winds and get involved with someone else. Someone who didn't *make sense*. She and Robbie are an item now. Did you know that?'

If Megan had intended to rile him with that dig then she

failed, because Alessandro simply shrugged and remarked evenly, 'I wish them well.'

A wave of hopelessness swept over her, leaving her small and defeated.

'What do you want me to say, Megan?' Alessandro had been enjoying life, enjoying whatever the hell she wanted to call it—their *relationship, situation, involvement*—but he wasn't enjoying being boxed into a corner. 'That I am prepared to make you promises which I know won't be fulfilled? Do you want to hear the whole love thing?' Every part of him that desired and saw the necessity for absolute control, rejected her directness.

'I never said that!'

'What, then?'

'You used me.'

Alessandro was outraged at that—outraged at her portrayal of herself as a passive victim when she had been as crazy for sex as he had.

However, he wasn't going to succumb to the weakness of raising his voice or getting emotional. 'If that's what you wish to believe, Megan, then there's nothing I can do to stop you. But just think about this: I came to you and you had every opportunity to tell me that you didn't want involvement. If I recall, you didn't do that. In fact, at no point did I get the impression that you wanted out. I might be mistaken…'

This time it was Megan's turn to fall silent as she considered the accuracy of that flatly intoned statement. Yes, he *had* given her the option of backing out.

'I was under the impression—'

'I never once told you that *I* had broken off my engagement with Victoria,' he reminded her, mercilessly driving home his point that she had not been coerced into any situation she hadn't wanted. 'You just went ahead and made assumptions.'

What he failed to tell her was that he would have broken it off with Victoria, anyway. Would have broken it off even if he *hadn't* found those mildly incriminating text messages on her mobile phone. Had been secretly relieved that the onus of ending their relationship hadn't fallen on his shoulders.

'And you never corrected those assumptions because they suited you. You wanted to get me into bed, and the fastest way of doing it was to lead me to believe that you had broken your engagement to Victoria.'

'I didn't need a fast way of doing that. We would have fallen into bed together anyway.' But he flushed, because there was a modicum of truth in what she was saying. He had known that, however much she was attracted to him, she would not have leapt into his arms had she thought for a passing minute that she was a plaything. He resented the fact that she was throwing all of this in his face when she could so easily have accepted the situation for what it was. Two people who had temporarily reconnected.

'Why?' Megan looked at him unblinkingly. 'Why did you bother? Why didn't you just leave me alone?'

'I realised that I still wanted you. I also realised that you still wanted *me*.'

'And so you thought…why not? Is that it?' Yet again, she was good enough to have a romp with, but not good enough for a committed relationship.

It seemed that neither of them had grown up after all. She was still looking for the impossible, and he was still convinced that she didn't fit the bill. The bitter truth, she thought, was that she fitted the bill even less now. In the space of seven years he had become so powerful that the concept of hitching his wagon to a woman who defiantly refused to obey him would be unthinkable.

'You think that you have somehow been insulted? What

you fail to understand is that what's happened between us *needed* to happen!'

Lost in a daze of her own agonising thoughts, Megan barely surfaced to hear his latest piece of wisdom.

Her brain caught up with what he was saying after a ten-second delay, and she looked at him blankly.

'What?'

'I am *saying*,' Alessandro repeated slowly, 'that we needed to get each other out of our systems. I am *saying* that the only way of doing that was to have a relationship, allow this over-powering mutual lust to burn itself out…'

Need? Lust? The words which she knew would have thrilled most women to death when applied to Alessandro dropped like poison into her consciousness.

While she had been blissfully toying with more romantic notions, he had summed everything up in an emotion that blew strong and then faded away. He had allowed her the illusion of pretending that there was more to what they had because he wanted to tire of her, and the only way he could do that was to have her until he no longer wanted her.

'You've said enough.' She forced her wooden body to move. 'I don't want to hear any more. I'm going to go upstairs and get my stuff now.' She reached for the ludicrously expensive jewellery adorning her and carefully removed it. 'You can have this back.'

'Don't be ridiculous.' A dark flush highlighted his sharp, arrogant cheekbones. 'What the hell am I going to do with women's jewellery?'

'I don't know and I don't care.' Since he was making no effort to take what she was offering him *back*, she casually dropped it on one of the side tables in the room. 'You can always give it to your next conquest. Most women adore this sort of thing.'

Alessandro watched her exit the room without fuss. No way was he going to follow her. He had a positive dislike of demanding women, and what could be more demanding than a woman who laid her cards on the table and threatened a walk-out unless her conditions were met?

He hadn't been lying when he had told her that he'd needed to get her out of his system. Whether she wanted to be realistic or not, he also hadn't been lying when he had told her that the same applied to her. If she wanted to ditch what they had, then so be it.

He decided that it just proved beyond the shadow of a doubt how much of a liability a woman like her was. She didn't accept things. She stridently made her opinions felt, even if she could see the opposition all around her. Did he need a woman like that in his life, however good the sex was?

He was assailed by a host of conflicting emotions, but when he tried to pin them down, he found that he couldn't. He could hear her rustling above him, collecting her things. There was a part of him that wanted to try and stop her, but of course, he wasn't going to fall victim to *that* pathetic instinct. Much more overwhelming was his sense of pride, and with pride came a gut-deep certainty that this was a narrow escape.

Finally he heard her half running down the stairs, and she reappeared in the doorway, once more in the clothes in which she had gone out shopping. The dress and all the other accessories had, he assumed, joined the discarded jewellery category.

'I won't tell you that you've blown this out of all proportion,' he heard himself say, in defiance of everything his head was telling him.

'You just did. And if that's your opinion, then you're welcome to voice it.'

'I think you're making a big mistake,' Alessandro said stiffly. For him, this felt like a major concession.

'Oh? And that would be…why? Exactly?'

'What are you going to do when you walk out of this house? Do you imagine that your life is going to slot back to the place it was before we happened to meet? Before we became lovers?'

'No. I don't think it will for a minute, Alessandro.'

Megan looked at him evenly. She was only now really appreciating how different he was from the man she had so stupidly fallen in love with seven years ago, and with whom she was now still so stupidly in love. Alessandro made love like a dream, and could make any woman feel like the sexiest woman on earth, but he was essentially a coldly logical man. He saw only the practicalities of marriage, and didn't shy away from an institution that would further enhance his standing. He was getting older, and how seriously could any man, however brilliant, intuitive and filthy rich, be taken by the People Who Mattered if he approached his forties still with the reputation of being a playboy? For someone whose work was his ruling passion, every scandalous inch in a gossip column would be seen as an erosion into his credibility.

Hence Victoria. She had been his perfect match, because she would never have interfered with his working life.

Realistically, Megan knew that she exercised some power over him—but only in a sexual sense. Her mistake had been to think that he would ever allow passion to rule his life. He hadn't seen her as enhancing his life, more as invading it, and everyone knew what happened to invaders. They were eventually repelled.

It was her misfortune that his role in her life was completely different. If he had been an invading force, then she had been a joyful captive, waving the white flag before he had even had the chance to take up residence. She hadn't so much surrendered before the first tank as begged to be taken on board.

'You said that we needed to get each other out of our

systems.' Megan smiled sadly. 'I think I can honestly say that I've done that. I've got the measure of you, and if my life doesn't go back to the place it was, then I'm hoping that it moves on to an even better place.'

'You've *got the measure of me*?' That sounded very much like criticism to Alessandro, and he was duly outraged. In fact, for the first time in his life he was rendered totally speechless. Not only had she thrown that uncalled-for insult at him, but she was now turning away, clearly seeing no need to follow through with the remark.

'At least,' she said, with a wry smile and one hand on the doorknob, 'there won't be any awkward moments at school. We won't bump into one another.'

For Megan, it had felt dignified to have the last word. She had also succeeded in not making a spectacle of herself. However, those two high points in the evening were lost over the next week or so, as reality set in with a vengeance.

She found it difficult to concentrate at school, and things were made worse when, only ten days after she had staged her walk-out on Alessandro, she was unhelpfully shown a centre spread in one of the tabloids by Charlotte. It featured an extremely riotous-looking Alessandro in the company of several beauties, all of whom were rich young things with family pedigrees coming out of their ears.

He might not be rushing to find another Victoria replacement, she thought bitterly, but he was certainly intent on enjoying himself on the way.

While she had been pining and rehashing their break-up in her head, to the point where she seemed to have a permanent headache, he had been out having fun. She had made her great long speech about putting him behind her and moving on to a better place, but actually all it had amounted to was *blah, blah, blah*.

'Okay.' She looked up from the newspaper to Charlotte, who had tactfully turned away and was reading instructions on the back of a packet of a microwave meal. 'You win. I'm going to get out there and start having some fun of my own.'

Charlotte immediately lost interest in the container in her hand and spun round with a broad grin.

'I know some clubs,' she said, reeling in her fish before it had time to wriggle off the hook. 'I can give you mellow and smoky—not literally, of course, with the smoking ban. Or I can give you *funky*, or upmarket classy… Take your pick.'

Megan, who had always enjoyed going out, and had always seen it as a cure-all for depression, wondered what her friend would say if she were to pick the option of staying in, yet again, with only her thoughts for company. She would probably, Megan thought, throw the microwave meal at her unresponsive head.

After a couple of days of sisterly-style sympathy, Charlotte had adopted the sergeant-major approach to the situation, with lots of bracing advice on moving forward and stirring suggestions on how that might be accomplished. To date Megan had steadfastly ignored them all, because she wanted to enjoy her misery, but now, seeing Alessandro in grainy black-and-white print, laughing, with a drink in one hand and the other hand round the waist of a brunette with legs to her armpits, she decided that it was time to dust herself down and at least make an effort to get on with her life.

'Anywhere,' she said, 'where there are no teenagers. The last thing I need is to feel old as well as miserable.'

'A qualified yes,' Charlotte said, rubbing her hands together in triumph, 'is better than no *yes* at all. We'll start with your hair….'

* * *

It was a form of being managed, and over the next few days, as a particularly hectic week of fractious children eased towards the weekend, Megan was surprisingly relieved to be taken in hand. She spent Saturday morning at the hairdressers, where Charlotte kept a watchful eye on what was being done to her hair like an anxious mother taking her only child for its first haircut. Then they went shopping, where she was made to try on clothes that she would have worn seven years previously but which had gradually morphed into more sensible outfits in keeping with her lifestyle.

'I'm not saying that you need to look like mutton dressed as lamb,' Charlotte assured her, 'but you're not exactly old, so anything in a dark colour, baggy, high-necked or mid-calf is out.'

'I can't afford all of this,' Megan protested half-heartedly.

'It's therapy,' Charlotte informed her, 'of the retail kind, and all therapy comes at a price. Believe me, Megan, the cost of a hairdo and an outfit is a whole lot cheaper than a couple of hours with a shrink….'

But not even an evening of clubbing—or three evenings of clubbing, for that matter—could relieve the dull ache inside her that seemed to be never-ending. Not that she confessed any of that to Charlotte, because her friend's efforts were valiant, and if they weren't entirely successful then it wasn't her fault.

When half-term began looming on the horizon, the week without demanding children that she usually anticipated so eagerly took on the aspect of a nightmare. Enforced leisure time which she didn't want.

Not that there weren't *some* avenues for enjoyment which she could usefully explore.

As an exercise for meeting guys—which was the foundation of much of Charlotte's strenuous efforts in getting her out of the house—the socialising scene hadn't been a total waste of time. True, the men she had met—friends of friends—

hadn't come close to having the sort of dynamic and immediate effect on her nervous system as Alessandro had. But that,
she assured herself, was a *good* thing. Remember the motto,
she told herself, about frying pans, fires and jumping!

Which was why, in the space of a couple of weeks, she had
actually gone out twice with her 'Pick of the Day', so to
speak—a lawyer called Stuart, who was a rising star in his
firm. He was a tall, good-looking man, with an easy smile and
a quiet, affable manner that didn't threaten her nervous system. They had been out once for a meal, which had been fun,
and once to the cinema, to see one of those chick flicks which
she would have had to have dragged Alessandro to see, kicking and screaming. Megan saw that as a very good omen. A
man who would voluntarily sit through a weepie must have
a core of sensitivity, and a sensitive man wasn't going to be
a heartbreaker.

The Friday before half-term, during which she had decided
to get away from London for a few days and clear her head
in the Lake District, staying at a B&B she had stayed at years
before, on her journey down to London, Stuart phoned to ask
her out again. Megan had no hesitation in accepting his invitation. She had already packed her overnight case, which was
waiting by the door for her to grab when she left in the morning, and having some fun with a guy who thought she was
bright and funny would be just the right start for a relaxing
week away from London.

She pulled one of her more glamorous outfits from the
batch which she had so optimistically bought when she had
been seeing Alessandro, which she had flung into a bin bag
and stuffed at the back of her wardrobe the second she'd
walked out on him. It was a pale blue dress which was de-
signed to be worn with other soft, falling layers above and
underneath, all belted at the waist. At the time it had seemed

a good investment, because layers could be added or subtracted according to the weather. Back then, she had been thinking *summer*. What a joke that now seemed! They hadn't even managed to leap into spring!

Stuart came promptly at seven-thirty, and was charmingly flattering about her outfit. He continued to flatter and cajole her into feeling happier than she had since she'd walked away from Alessandro. By ten-thirty, when they arrived back at her house, she felt at ease about accepting the lips that met hers.

But the kiss wasn't electrifying. Not like... *No! She wasn't going to go there!* She wrapped her arms around his neck and really, really tried to inject some passion into returning his kiss. But her mouth wouldn't oblige, and when he stepped away from her there was a rueful smile on his face.

'Not working, is it, Megan?' Stuart said.

'It might. In time.'

'And pigs might fly. In time.' He brushed her cheek gently with one finger. 'Actually, in time but with another guy. I'd wait around, because you're the kind of girl a man *would* wait around for, but somehow I don't think I'll ever fit the bill. So...friends...?'

'Sure. Friends!'

Friends. She could foresee the years stretching ahead, during which time she would make lots and lots of *friends* and always end up the bridesmaid but never the bride.

And who did she have to blame? Herself. Alessandro had ripped her life apart twice, and she couldn't help but think that whilst once could be excused as an unfortunate event, twice bordered on downright reckless.

And Stuart would have been such a good catch! She kissed him regretfully on the cheek, and then hugged him before waving him off in the direction of the underground.

The house was dark and quiet without Charlotte around.

Megan went to the kitchen, and was gazing thoughtfully at the kettle while it boiled when she heard the sharp peal of the doorbell. Now that Stuart had gone, having had quite a touching farewell, she was a little irritated that he might have returned for a repeat performance. She chastised herself for being so harsh. He was a nice guy, and if he wanted to carry on chatting for a while then she would welcome him in.

She pulled open the door with a smile pinned on her face— and her mouth fell open at the sight of Alessandro, standing on her doorstep. She had been thinking of him only minutes before, as she had waited for the kettle to boil, and she had to blink to dispel the illusion that her feverish imagination had conjured up a ghost.

'I seem to make a habit of turning up on your doorstep,' Alessandro told her wryly, breaking the spell. 'A bit like a stray. I've been trying to work out why that is.'

His inclination was to push past her, get inside the house, demand to find out who the guy was he had seen with her outside only ten minutes before, the guy she had been kissing on the mouth, but he hung back. For starters, since when was it acceptable for an ex to be lurking outside his girlfriend's house, spying? For another, since when did *he*, a man who could have any woman he wanted, *ever* do something as weird as that?

But Alessandro had pretty much given up on finding answers to his behaviour as far as Megan was concerned. The past few weeks had been hellish. He had done his utmost to take the reins by getting out there, reminding himself that there were plenty other fish in the sea. But not only had the plentiful fish been spectacularly disappointing, he had not even been tempted to sample any.

Was this love? He didn't know. He had just reached a point

when he knew that he had to see her. And he had. With another man. Kissing him. But he wouldn't go there.

The knowledge that he might be too late, that she might have moved on, hit him in a tidal rush of urgent panic.

No, he definitely wouldn't mention the other guy, because that would be certain to get her back up and right now Alessandro just wanted to win some Brownie points.

'Forget it.' It took enormous strength to say that, but Megan was rapidly making an assessment of the situation.

Alessandro had been out partying and having fun, had maybe—no, *probably*—slept with some of those beauties she had seen in the newspaper, hanging on to his arm for dear life, but she was still on his mind. And for all the wrong reasons. Sex, lust, unfinished business—not to mention a healthy dollop of flattened male pride because *she* had been the one to do the walking this time. He hadn't had his chance to get sick of her, and now he was back to finish what he had started.

She began closing the door, but he inserted himself neatly into the open space, and pushing against him was like pushing against the Rock of Gibraltar. Megan gave up and glared at him.

'Didn't you hear what I said, Alessandro?' she asked tightly. 'I don't want to see you. I've said everything I wanted to say and I've moved on with my life now.'

Moved on with another man. It was like a punch in the gut. He wondered whether she and the guy had got round to sleeping together yet, and the thought of it sent a red haze of rage through his mind.

'And you've moved on with yours,' she couldn't resist adding.

'What are you talking about?'

'Nothing.' She tried to inch the door shut, but he pushed against it and stepped into the hallway. He didn't know what it was, but this woman drove him to the brink of madness.

'You can't make a statement like that and then refuse to qualify it.'

'You know what I'm talking about!'

Now that he was finally inside, Alessandro felt less like a man teetering on the edge of a precipice. At least he had her full attention. 'I don't.'

'In which case you're stupid. But we both know you're not that!' Megan pressed herself against the wall, her hands behind her back, her eyes blazing with defiant anger. 'I saw all those pictures of you plastered in the newspapers.'

She knew as soon as the words were out of her mouth that he didn't have a clue what she was talking about. He had never, even at university, read the tabloids. He had only ever read the broadsheets. Nothing had changed, and she could have kicked herself for opening herself.

'What pictures?'

Megan took a deep breath and looked at him scornfully. 'Pictures of you having a riotous time with a bevy of beautiful women. And I don't have any objection to that,' she bit out, 'because we're no longer together. In fact, *I've* been having a riotous time of my own, as a matter of fact.' She thought of Stuart and the *riotous time* she had had kissing him and trying to kid herself that it hadn't felt like kissing a slab of wood.

Alessandro felt his spirits soar with satisfaction that she had been following his movements, had been jealous of the women with whom he had pointlessly tried to have a good time. It felt great—until he thought about the riotous time she claimed *she* had been having. Then he crashed back down to earth with supersonic speed.

'You shouldn't read those trashy newspapers,' he gritted. 'And you should know better than to believe that they ever report the truth.'

'Meaning what?' Megan flung at him.

'Meaning that I went out, sure, but if you thought from what you saw that I was having a good time, then you were wrong.'

'Guess what? I don't believe you.' But she *wanted* to.

'I can't blame you.'

Alessandro raked his fingers through his hair and looked at her with unrestrained frustration. He could manipulate any opportunity, had ruthlessly practised the art in many a board-room, but just at the moment he felt like a man in a strait-jacket, desperately struggling to find a way out so that he could swim to shore.

'Look, can we at least go and sit down?'

He could see her struggling with the question, and for a few seconds he wondered what he would do if she refused—if this brand-new life she had apparently found had been a stepping stone for her to move out of his orbit. He cursed himself for not having been more relentless in his pursuit. As it stood, he had let her go, and in so doing had given her a window of op-portunity to find herself a replacement.

'I don't see the point,' Megan told him.

'Why?' Natural aggression flowed into Alessandro's veins and he shoved his hands in his pockets. He could feel his resolve to take things easy disappearing fast, like smoke in a high wind.

'Why would I sit down with you when I want you to leave?'

'I should never have let you walk away!'

'You didn't *let* me walk away, Alessandro!' Megan cried. 'I walked away because I *wanted* to!'

'Don't say that!'

'It's the truth.'

'No! The truth is that I...I would have finished with Victoria even if I hadn't found out that there was a third party involved. Or should I say a third party who was *trying* to get involved. I would have finished with her because you were in my head and I wanted to be with you. So you see, Megan, the fact is that my choice would have been for you, but for a mistake in timing.'

'I don't believe you.' Too many disappointments had taken their toll, and Megan looked at him bitterly.

'Then what *do* you believe?'

She drew in one deep, unsteady breath, and her eyes didn't waver as she looked at him, drawing deep from her reserves of courage because even now, after everything, looking at him still made her feel sick and giddy with love. He had said that he had flung himself into having fun, but that he hadn't found the fun he'd thought he would. She believed him. He didn't look like a man who had been out having a good time. In fact, he looked wrecked.

'I think that you do still want me, Alessandro. But I'm not going to bother going down the road of trying to figure out whether what you want is a relationship or not. It doesn't matter. You want me because you know that sooner or later you'll get tired of me, and when that happens you'll be free to move on.'

'And what would you say if I told you that I don't *want* to move on?'

Megan looked at his face, unusually hesitant, and then nodded towards the sitting room.

'Ten minutes.'

Alessandro hadn't realised how tense he had been until he exhaled a deep breath of relief and preceded her into the sitting room, removing his coat en route and resting it on a side table.

'Where's Charlotte?' he asked.

'Out.'

'Is she going away somewhere?'

'Why do you ask?' He had made himself at home on one of the sofas, but Megan still found it hard to relax, and had remained by the door, her arms folded, her defences ready to slam into place at the slightest hint of trouble.

'I noticed a suitcase by the door.'

'That's my case. I'm going away for the half-term week.'

'Your case…'

His mind played with the notion that she might not be going away on her own. Until now he had had an arrogant faith in her dependability on him. Even when they had met again, had resumed their relationship, he had still known that however much she might have hankered for something more she had not been looking around. Now he wasn't too sure. But he shut the door on that meandering, unpleasant thought.

'Whatever you believed about my motivations,' Alessandro said in a raw undertone, 'you were wrong. I've tried to put you out of my mind but I can't, and I want more of you than just an occasional relationship. I know that you're still hankering for a country life, and I have realised that what you want has a pretty high priority in my life. So let's do it, Megan….'

Megan held her breath while frantic hope beat inside her like a drum.

'Let's move in together. A house in the country. Wherever you want.' He hadn't felt dizzy like this when he had contemplated marrying Victoria. For some reason he felt like a man taking a plunge into waters unknown. 'But let's do it soon.'

CHAPTER NINE

ALESSANDRO looked at Megan over the *Financial Times*. She was sitting cross-legged on the sofa, absorbed in a cookery programme. A celebrity chef was giving her tips on how to cook a dish which he knew she would never attempt.

Their move to the country hadn't been quite as dramatic as he had anticipated. She had wanted to still be able to travel to her work, and so they had moved to one of the leafier suburbs of central London, from which she could reach her school on the tube every day. The street was lined with trees, and he had got his people to hunt down the closest he could get to her dream house. It was Grade II listed, with the requisite white fence with roses, and original stained-glass features inside.

Two months ago he had seen this as a highly suitable arrangement. He would have her living with him and his work life would remain largely uninterrupted. His house in central London was empty, and although he had briefly contemplated selling it, he had quickly discarded the idea. It wasn't as though he needed the money.

Now, two months on, he discovered that his work life wasn't what it used to be. He enjoyed being with her, and didn't care to think of her sitting on her own in the house, so he had found himself voluntarily ending his day at a reasonable time so that he could return home. He had even taken to delegating his overseas trips to one of his trusted company directors.

She had asked for none of that. In fact, he thought, looking at her rapt expression as she watched the television, she had demanded nothing from him. He should have been pleased with that, but increasingly he was finding that he wasn't.

He also didn't like the fact that she kept in touch with the loser he had seen her kissing on her doorstep the night he had asked her to move in with him.

It seemed that he was one of Charlotte's friends, and occasionally a crowd of them went out after work for drinks. She made no effort to conceal the fact, and he believed her when she assured him, after some very light questioning, that the man was a nice person and a friend, and they'd both accepted that they were not suited for a relationship.

Alessandro still didn't like it. He wanted her exclusively to himself—by which he meant that he didn't want her to look at another man, talk to another man, far less be *buddies* with another man. Whom she had kissed. It suggested to him that she wasn't giving herself *entirely* to him and he couldn't help wondering if there was a part of her still on the look-out. Had he hurt her so much that he had killed something between them? She was never anything but happy in his company, but niggling doubts were tearing him apart.

He flung the newspaper on the ground. 'You're never going to make that dish, Megan,' he said, shutting the door on the disturbing drift of his thoughts.

'I know, but I live in hope that I might be inspired.' Megan turned to him and grinned. 'It's crazy to have your chef prepare stuff all the time when I'm perfectly capable of cooking. Well, at least of using a recipe book. Now and again.' She went across to him on the sofa, which was a long, very deep, squashy one, quite unlike the cold leather furniture in his Chelsea house.

He was wearing low-slung casual trousers, the ones that had a delicious habit of slipping down his hips, revealing the tightly packed muscles of his torso. Familiarity with his body had done nothing to diminish her craving for him, and she ran her hands over his chest, curling against his body and sighing with pleasure when he pushed his hand under her tee shirt and absentmindedly began caressing her breast. Her nipple predictably tightened into a tight, responsive bud, and she feverishly yanked off the tee shirt, laying herself open to his hungry, dark eyes.

If nothing else, the one thing she knew for sure was that he was greedy for her. Their lovemaking was intense and deeply, deeply satisfying. Right now she wanted him to suckle her nipple, to slip his hand under her panties to where she was hot and wet for him, to send that wonderful fire racing through her veins until she felt giddy and wonderfully out of control.

So much was so good, and this most of all. Two months of pure happiness—although in her quiet moments Megan wondered. He had committed so much, but not once had he even hinted that his commitment might go further. Something held her back. He had never, even in moments of great passion, when every barrier he possessed came tumbling down as his orgasm shuddered through his big body, uttered those three words, *I love you*. Sometimes she figured that there was enough love in her for both of them—although she never let on what she felt, and nor did she ever ask anything of him, mindful of that trait of emotional self-sufficiency which he had found so appealing in Victoria.

Other times, however, there was a dark, destructive voice that reminded her that they might be living together but he still hadn't got rid of his house in Chelsea. She hadn't asked him why that was, and she occasionally wondered whether it was because the bigger part of him, the part that wasn't all wrapped up in touching her, was conscious of the fact that they probably wouldn't remain together. Why ditch his house when he thought he would move back into it sooner or later?

In accepting his offer to move in with him Megan had resigned herself to a life always lived for the moment. With that in mind, she made sure to carry on with her social life, ignoring his frowning disapproval whenever she announced that she would be getting back late. She had also found a firm friend in Stuart, who had slipped into the spot Robbie had held, as a male confidant in whom she had absolute trust. She made sure that she hung on to him—also in the face of Alessandro's frowning disapproval.

In that uncertain place she occupied she would give up a lot, but not everything.

'That feels good.' She sighed, and parted her legs, inviting him to do what he wanted.

Instead, she felt his hand smooth her thigh and resolutely tuck her legs neatly together—which made her sit bolt-upright, because Alessandro, unpredictable in so many ways, was always completely predictable when it came to sex.

'What's the matter?' She drew her legs up and wrapped her arms around them.

'Bad news, I'm afraid. I have to go away on business for a couple of days.'

The surge of bitter disappointment reminded Megan of just how much she had invested in what they had. She had begun to take for granted his daily presence in her life, never once questioning how it was that a workaholic had suddenly become so domesticated. But things would change, and she wondered whether this was the start of it.

'Don't be silly.' She forced a smile. 'Why is that bad news? I do understand that you have an empire to run, you know. As a matter of fact…' she thought quickly, making sure to wriggle out

of the box labelled *clingy*, which was anathema to Alessandro
'…it's been ages since I met up with all my friends…'

'Ten days.'

'Ten days? Are you sure?'

Oh, Alessandro was sure, all right. She had gone out for a
pizza, and amongst their number had been the *good friend*
whatever-his-name-was. Alessandro had chosen *not* to
actively store that information in his brain.

He was growing more irritable by the second. Was he mistaken, or did she sound *pleased* that she was going to be
having a bit of time to herself? He decided to test the water.
Yes, he had to be away for two nights—which could easily
be extended to four, because there was always a bank of
clients with whom he could usefully meet—but really, he
wanted to hurry back to her.

'Actually, it's more like four nights. New York.'

To Megan, four nights sounded like eternity.

'Lucky you!' she trilled. 'I've always wanted to go to New
York! I don't suppose there's much point asking, but try and
take some pictures!'

'You could come with me.' He had never asked a woman
to go on a business trip with him—even a business trip which
he had only contrived to lengthen on the spur of the moment.

'No chance. School.'

Alessandro scowled. 'A few days away wouldn't result in
a generation of drop-outs.'

'True. But I can't.' There was an edginess to his mood that
was transmitting itself to her.

'Who are you going to go out with?'

'Oh, just a few friends. Probably a pub.'

That said nothing. Alessandro's mood deteriorated and
later, when they made love, there was an aggression that only
stopped a little short of savagery.

He told her that he would call. Every day. Megan told him that there was no need, that she would be fine. She was determined to show him self-reliance.

He left for the airport with the ridiculous notion that he had stupidly dug himself a hole by telling her that he would be away at least two days longer than he needed to be.

It left him a hell of a lot of time to wonder whether she would be going out and chatting with the guy she seemed determined to hang on to even though she must *know* that it just wasn't on. At least not in *his* world.

He couldn't concentrate. He repeatedly told himself that it had been a stupid idea to try and tease a response out of her by absenting himself from the scene. And she didn't seem herself when he called her.

Alessandro, who had an office in Manhattan, in one of the seriously tall buildings that dwarfed the street below, swung round in his chair and glared out of the floor-to-ceiling sheet of glass that separated him from a twenty-storey free fall.

He had just got off the phone to her, and although the time difference might have excused her subdued and downright weird response to hearing his voice, he had the sickening feeling that something was wrong.

On the spur of the moment he snatched up the telephone again, drummed his fingers restlessly on the desk as the telephone exchange did its business and connected him through to the landline at the house once again.

It took for ever for her to take the call, making him wonder what he had been interrupting and throwing him into an even darker mood.

'What's the matter?' he delivered tightly, cutting to the chase.

'Matter?' Several thousand miles away, Megan swallowed hard as she bought some time. Of course she should have known that Alessandro would have caught her change of mood. Even when he wasn't looking at her he still seemed capable of reading her like a book.

'Something's wrong. What is it?'

'Nothing. Well…actually, nothing's *wrong*, as such, but… but we need to talk…when you get back…'

'Talk? Talk about what?' Alessandro had bad experiences with Megan's *need to talk* pronouncements, and he was getting a bad feeling now. Suddenly all the meetings he had lined up faded into inconsequence. He would leave New York immediately. He would buy a bloody jet if he had to in order to accomplish that.

'Don't worry, Alessandro…it can wait.'

'Are you sure?'

'Absolutely.'

Wait? She just wished it could wait for ever. She held up the little plastic stick with the prominent positive pregnancy line stamped on it like the decisive hand of fate. A bit of sickness, tenderness in her breasts… It hadn't occurred to her that she might be pregnant until the evening Alessandro had left for New York. She had visited Charlotte for dinner, and after a second dash to the bathroom because she'd felt a little queasy had had the idea planted in her head, when her friend had jokingly asked whether there was 'a bun in the oven'.

Naturally they had been using contraception. Alessandro had taken care of that. But there had been a couple of times when lust had overridden care. And, thinking back, when had she seen her last period anyway? She had always had irregular periods. That absence, in the great scheme of things, hadn't been noticed.

'Don't worry about me,' she told Alessandro now. 'You have fun over there in New York.'

'*Have fun?* I'm here on business, Megan. What the hell do you imagine I'm getting up to?'

'I have no idea,' Megan said waspishly. 'It's your concern!' Tears were gathering at the back of her throat. 'Anyway, I'll see you when you get back, in a couple of days.' At which point she hung up.

He would probably be furious at that, she thought. He would see it as a gesture of defiance—which it hadn't been.

His reaction to the phone call, however, was taking second place to the dilemma raging inside her. All the doubts she had shoved away had crept out of their hiding places and were wreaking long-overdue havoc.

The minute Alessandro found out about this pregnancy he would insist she marry him. After all this time Megan knew him well enough to know that he was a man who was not afraid of committing for the right reasons. Or at least the right reasons *for him*. For reasons that *made sense*. Hence his engagement to Victoria. *She* had made sense. Hence his living with her. It made *sense* to expunge her by having her rather than fight it. A baby would necessitate marriage. That, to him, would make *sense*, because no child of his would be born out of wedlock.

Megan could envisage the Victorian speech even as she sat with the phone in her hand, staring at it.

Did she want to be married to a man who didn't love her? She had agreed to move in with him because she hadn't been able to envisage life without him, because at the back of her mind there had been a thread of hope that she would eventually be able to win him over. But would she be able to face a lifetime knowing that he had married her for the wrong reasons? Connected by a child and in a position where walking away might become an impossibility?

For the first time since she had started her job Megan took the next day off work.

With the silence of an empty house around her, she had

time to really sit down and take stock. Alessandro disliked emotional roller-coaster rides. She had been too much for him seven years ago, and she had tried very hard not to make any demands of him since she had moved in with him. She had never questioned his movements and had maintained her independence. Fat lot of good all *that* had done when he was about to be flung onto the craziest roller-coaster ride of his life. She wondered whether he would resent her for having catapulted him into a situation he would never in a million years have wanted with her. Thinking about that made her feel even sicker than she already felt.

The miserable grey day faded into gathering nightfall, and she drooped around the house, ignoring all phone calls and making sure to switch off her cellphone—because Alessandro would phone again, and she just needed time without hearing his voice.

She hadn't expected to see him. Not when he should have been thousands of miles away. And she was lying on the sofa in the sitting room, nursing the start of a headache, when she felt rather than heard his sudden presence in the room.

He was standing in the doorway and she wondered how long he had been there, looking at her with the strangest expression on his face. The least he could have done was announce his presence by making some noise!

Megan scrambled into a sitting position, the onset of her headache forgotten as she absorbed the deeply sexy man around whom she now felt she had spent *years* orbiting, like a lost little planet trying to fight a gravitational pull that was too powerful for her.

'Wha…what are you doing back here?'

Alessandro looked at her white stricken face and knew that he had been right to have dropped everything and returned.

'You said that you wanted to talk.'

'You flew back here because I said that we needed to *talk*?'

Alessandro was quick to spot the fact that she had replaced *wanted* with *needed*.

'I'm glad,' he asserted, moving towards her.

Before he had left for New York she had been all over him. Now she was watching him cautiously, and he felt a film of perspiration break out over his body. He didn't know what had engineered this change but time apart, not to mention long, hellish hours on the Red-Eye, had put everything into perspective.

'Because I want to talk too.' He swung his long body onto the sofa with her but maintained a certain distance, because he didn't want to be distracted by the proximity of her body. She was looking at him, holding her breath, and Alessandro wondered why it had taken him so long to wake up to the obvious. 'I've been a fool,' he muttered in a low, raw voice, which meant that she had to lean towards him just to catch what he was saying. 'We should never have been apart.'

'You had meetings in New York….'

'That's not what I'm talking about,' he said, waving aside her interruption with an impatient gesture that was so eloquently *him*. 'I mean…' There was a confusing jumble of words inside him, and a panicky desperation for her to hear them. 'Seven years ago…I made a mistake…'

'You did?'

'I was a young, ambitious fool.' He was facing up to a stark truth which he had known from the very first minute she had walked out of his digs at the university, and it felt good to get it off his chest. 'I thought I knew what I wanted.'

'You were never a fool. Maybe young and ambitious, but never a fool.'

'I was a fool to let you walk away from me.' His dark, mesmeric eyes held hers, and Megan felt her heart swoop. This was hardly the conversation she had envisaged, but she was liking it, and hungry to discover where it would lead.

'I thought…'

Alessandro paused, travelling back to a time when he had figured he knew all the answers. From the fluctuations and vagaries of living hand to mouth he would have a life over which he could exercise control—a life which would leave no room for the unpredictable. Megan had been unpredictable. That had been his plan.

'I thought…' He refocused on her. 'I thought that you weren't what I needed. I…I grew up seeing my parents struggle with poverty. It was their constant companion. I was determined never to find myself caught in the same trap, and I thought that the only way to avoid it was to accumulate enough power and wealth to make me invincible. Only then could I be happy. I was wrong. Power and wealth don't bring happiness, and the idea of being in control of every aspect of your life is an illusion. And thank God for that. The thing is, I forgot the one thing I should have had branded in my head from my parents. They might have been broke but they were happy. You were always there, Megan, at the back of my mind and in my heart, and now…'

He shook his head, as if mystified by the inaccurate assumptions he had made. 'I can't live without you,' he told her simply. 'I tried to wrap it all up in something that made sense and I didn't stop to think that when it comes to you—' this time he smiled crookedly '—it's all about winging it. It's not supposed to make sense.' He took her fingers in his hand and idly played with them. 'I know you want to talk about us…maybe tell me that you're having second thoughts about this situation…'

He didn't dare say what else he had thought—that maybe she might want to tell him that he had messed her around just a little too much, that living with him had perhaps opened up her eyes to the fact that she valued her freedom more than she valued his continual presence in her life as a man who refused to commit any further than he thought strictly necessary. Maybe—and this had been the darkest fear of all—she had wanted to tell him that she would rather work on the loser who would probably stick a ring on her finger after the second date than stay around for the man who had resolutely refused to.

Megan was guiltily aware that when it came to second-guessing her motivations he wasn't precisely on cue, but that confession about his childhood had left her breathless. She had only ever had snippets of information about his background, and in a strange way she felt as though a barrier had been breached.

'I don't want to lose you,' Alessandro told her urgently. 'You think I'm a bad bet, but I'm not. I'm...' A *good* bet? Having pretty much told her that he only wanted her around so that he could get her out of his system? Was there a brain cell in his head? 'I'm in love with you, and you can't even think of leaving me.'

'You're in love with me?'

'I think I always have been.'

'You've never, ever said...' Megan was trembling as she looked at his starkly vulnerable face. She felt a lifetime of love swell inside her, and she touched his cheek as if discovering it for the first time.

'Like I said, I was a fool.' He trapped her hand in his and held it tightly. 'I never stopped to ask myself how it was that work became secondary the minute you appeared on the scene. You make me lose focus.'

'And that's a good thing?' Megan asked tremulously.

'It's a very good thing. It's the best thing I've ever known.'

'Are you sure?'

The look he gave her answered that question, and she smiled, her face lit up with joy.

'Because I love you too. I never stopped. Why do you think I agreed to move in with you? It went against reason, but you make me feel…helpless….'

'And that's just the way I like it,' Alessandro told her with immense satisfaction. There was a lot more that he wanted to tell her, and he knew that he would, in time. For the moment he was content to revel in the perfection of the moment. 'But I'd like it even more if you tell me now that you'll be my wife.'

'Yes!' She drew his head towards her and kissed him, and only when she at last opened her eyes once again did she remember why she had needed to talk to him. How on earth could she have forgotten something that had consumed her for the past three days?

'I'm so happy,' she whispered. 'Because…'

'Because…?' Oh, yes, she wanted to have a talk. But Alessandro knew himself to be unassailable. 'You told me on the phone that you wanted to talk to me…?'

'I do…and brace yourself for a bit of a shock… You're going to be a father….'

'I still think that you tricked me when you got me catching the first flight from New York because you wanted to *talk*,' Alessandro told her several months later, as he gazed at her lying next to him in the bed, with their beautiful baby daughter between them. 'You had me worried sick that I might be losing you, and here I am. Not only do I have you, my darling, but I have this miracle lying between us.'

Isabella, whose name they had promptly shortened to Bella, caught his finger and instantly drew it to her mouth.

'If only I was that clever. I would have pulled that trick a lot earlier.' Megan smiled.

It was nearly a year now, and each day was better than the one before. They still lived in the house they had bought in leafy London, and she had continued working right up to the last possible moment—even though he had fussed and fretted like a mother hen, and would have wrapped her in cotton wool for the duration of her pregnancy if he could have. She had stood her ground—something which she now did, safe in the knowledge that it was just one of the things he loved about her. Even more of a revelation had been his admission that he loved her when she was argumentative and stubborn, and he had also told her that if she wasn't possessive with him then he might just be inclined to feel unloved.

So now Megan was the person she was, never hiding anything of herself or editing her personality in any way.

She had even begun buying him the occasional wild item of clothing—and he, a further miracle, had actually worn a few.

'You could, of course, do it again.' He reached across to stroke her face, his dark eyes tender. 'I think it's time I came home and you surprised me with the news that there's another little Bella on the way…'

'Because you're still aiming for that football team…?'

He grinned at her, and they laughed, and Bella's eyes flew open so that she could deliver a glaring reprimand to them both for waking her up.

A private joke. They shared lots of those now, but this one was the dearest held. For Robbie and Victoria had been married around the same time as they had, and they had been the ones to move out to the country, where Victoria had taken up a much less stressed job working for a small firm of lawyers, spending lots of time with Dominic. Right now she was pregnant, with a brother or sister for Dominic, and Robbie had been rash enough to bet that he would be coaching his own personal football team before Alessandro. Something which Megan and Victoria had found very amusing, considering *they* would be the ones giving birth to those amazing prodigies-to-be.

'I would never dare to suggest such a thing, my darling…'
He leant across to kiss her on the lips—a feathery kiss that
made her tummy flutter.

'But you're crazy enough to.'

Yes, he thought. This was his life and he loved it. Crazy,
in the end, made sense.

* * * * *

*Harlequin Presents® is thrilled
to introduce a sexy new duet,*
HOT BED OF SCANDAL, *by Kelly Hunter!*
Read on for a sneak peek of the first book
EXPOSED: MISBEHAVING WITH THE MAGNATE.

'I'M ATTRACTED to you and don't see why I should deny it. Our
kiss in the garden suggests you're not exactly indifferent to
me. The solution seems fairly straightforward.'

'You want me to become the comte's convenient mistress?'

'I'm not a comte,' Luc said. 'All I have is the castle.'

'All right, the billionaire's preferred plaything, then.'

'I'm not a billionaire, either. Yet.' His lazy smile warned
her it was on his to-do list. 'No, I want you to become my outrageously beautiful, independently wealthy lover.'

'Isn't that the same option?'

'No, you might have noticed that the wording's a little
different.'

'They're just words, Luc. The outcome's the same.'

'It's an attitude thing.' He looked at her, his smile crookedly
charming. 'So what do you say?'

To an affair with the likes of Luc Duvalier? 'I say it's dangerous. For both of us.'

Luc's eyes gleamed. 'There is that.'

'Not to mention insane.'

'Quite possibly. Was that a yes?'

Gabrielle really didn't know what to say. 'So how do

we start this thing? If I were to agree to it. Which I haven't.' Yet.

'We start with dinner. Tonight. No expectations beyond a pleasant evening with fine food, fine wine and good company. And we see what happens.'

'I don't know,' she said, reaching for her coffee. 'It seems a little…'

'Straightforward?' he suggested. 'Civilized?'

'For us, yes,' she murmured. 'Where would we eat? Somewhere public or in private?'

'Somewhere public,' he said firmly. 'The restaurant I'm thinking of is a fine one—excellent food, small premises and always busy. A man might take his lover there if he was trying to keep his hands off her.'

'Would I meet you there?' she said.

'I will, of course, collect you,' he said, playing the autocrat and playing it well. 'Shall I meet you there,' he murmured in disbelief. 'What kind of question is that?'

'Says the new generation Frenchman,' she countered. 'Liberated, egalitarian, nonsexist…'

'Helpful, attentive, chivalrous…' he added with a reckless smile. 'And very beddable.'

He was that.

'All right,' she said. 'I'll give you the day—and tonight— to prove that a civilized, pleasurable and manageable affair wouldn't be beyond us. If you can prove this to my satisfaction, I'll make love with you. If this gets out of hand, however…'

'Yes?' he said silkily. 'What do you suggest?'

Gabrielle leaned forward, elbows on the table. Luc

leaned forward, too. 'Well, I don't know about you,' she murmured, 'but I'm a clever, outrageously beautiful, independently wealthy woman. I plan to run.'

This sparky story is full of passion, wit and scandal and will leave you wanting more!
Look for
EXPOSED: MISBEHAVING WITH THE MAGNATE
Available March 2010

Two families torn apart by secrets and desire
are about to be reunited in

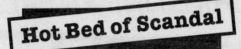

a sexy new duet by

Kelly Hunter

EXPOSED: MISBEHAVING WITH THE MAGNATE

#2905 Available March 2010

Gabriella Alexander returns to the French vineyard she
was banished from after being caught in flagrante with the
owner's son Lucien Duvalier–only to finish what they started!

REVEALED: A PRINCE AND A PREGNANCY

#2913 Available April 2010

Simone Duvalier wants Rafael Alexander and always has, but
they both get more than they bargained for when a night of
passion and a royal revelation rock their world!

www.eHarlequin.com

HP12905

SPECIAL EDITION

FROM *USA TODAY* BESTSELLING AUTHOR
CHRISTINE RIMMER

A BRIDE FOR JERICHO BRAVO

Marnie Jones had long ago buried her wild-child impulses and opted to be "safe," romantically speaking. But one look at born rebel Jericho Bravo and she began to wonder if her thrill-seeking side was about to be revived. Because if ever there was a man worth taking a chance on, there he was, right within her grasp....

*Available in March
wherever books are sold.*

THE WESTMORELANDS

NEW YORK TIMES
bestselling author

BRENDA JACKSON

HOT WESTMORELAND NIGHTS

Ramsey Westmoreland knew better than to lust
after the hired help. But Chloe, the new cook,
was just so delectable. Though their affair was
growing steamier, Chloe's motives became
suspicious. And when he learned Chloe was
carrying his child this Westmoreland Rancher
had to choose between pride or duty.

Available March 2010 wherever books are sold.

Always Powerful, Passionate and Provocative.

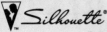

LARGER-PRINT BOOKS!

HARLEQUIN *Presents*

PASSION GUARANTEED SEDUCTION

GET 2 FREE LARGER-PRINT NOVELS PLUS 2 FREE GIFTS!

YES! Please send me 2 FREE LARGER-PRINT Harlequin Presents® novels and my 2 FREE gifts (gifts are worth about $10). After receiving them, if I don't wish to receive any more books, I can return the shipping statement marked "cancel." If I don't cancel, I will receive 6 brand-new novels every month and be billed just $4.55 per book in the U.S. or $5.24 per book in Canada. That's a saving of 13% off the cover price! It's quite a bargain! Shipping and handling is just 50¢ per book in the U.S. and 75¢ per book in Canada.* I understand that accepting the 2 free books and gifts places me under no obligation to buy anything. I can always return a shipment and cancel at any time. Even if I never buy another book, the two free books and gifts are mine to keep forever.

176 HDN E4GC   376 HDN E4GN

Name _____ (PLEASE PRINT) _____

Address _____ Apt. # _____

City _____ State/Prov. _____ Zip/Postal Code _____

Signature (if under 18, a parent or guardian must sign) _____

Mail to the **Harlequin Reader Service:**
IN U.S.A.: P.O. Box 1867, Buffalo, NY 14240-1867
IN CANADA: P.O. Box 609, Fort Erie, Ontario L2A 5X3

Not valid for current subscribers to Harlequin Presents Larger-Print books.

**Are you a subscriber to Harlequin Presents books
and want to receive the larger-print edition?
Call 1-800-873-8635 today!**

* Terms and prices subject to change without notice. Prices do not include applicable taxes. Sales tax applicable in N.Y. Canadian residents will be charged applicable provincial taxes and GST. Offer not valid in Quebec. This offer is limited to one order per household. All orders subject to approval. Credit or debit balances in a customer's account(s) may be offset by any other outstanding balance owed by or to the customer. Please allow 4 to 6 weeks for delivery. Offer available while quantities last.

Your Privacy: Harlequin Books is committed to protecting your privacy. Our Privacy Policy is available online at www.eHarlequin.com or upon request from the Reader Service. From time to time we make our lists of customers available to reputable third parties who may have a product or service of interest to you. If you would prefer we not share your name and address, please check here. ☐

Help us get it right—We strive for accurate, respectful and relevant communications. To clarify or modify your communication preferences, visit us at www.ReaderService.com/consumerschoice.

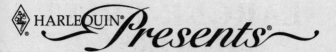

Devastating, dark-hearted and...
looking for brides.

Look for

BOUGHT:
DESTITUTE YET DEFIANT
by *Sarah Morgan*
#2902

From the lowliest slums to Millionaire's Row...
these men have everything now but their brides—
and they'll settle for nothing less than the best!

**Available March 2010
from Harlequin Presents!**